THE
JOURNEY
PRIZE

STORIES

WINNERS OF THE $10,000 JOURNEY PRIZE

1989: Holley Rubinsky for "Rapid Transits"

1990: Cynthia Flood for "My Father Took a Cake to France"

1991: Yann Martel for "The Facts Behind the Helsinki Roccamatios"

1992: Rozena Maart for "No Rosa, No District Six"

1993: Gayla Reid for "Sister Doyle's Men"

1994: Melissa Hardy for "Long Man the River"

1995: Kathryn Woodward for "Of Marranos and Gilded Angels"

1996: Elyse Gasco for "Can You Wave Bye Bye, Baby?"

1997 (shared): Gabriella Goliger for "Maladies of the Inner Ear"
    Anne Simpson for "Dreaming Snow"

1998: John Brooke for "The Finer Points of Apples"

1999: Alissa York for "The Back of the Bear's Mouth"

2000: Timothy Taylor for "Doves of Townsend"

2001: Kevin Armstrong for "The Cane Field"

2002: Jocelyn Brown for "Miss Canada"

2003: Jessica Grant for "My Husband's Jump"

2004: Devin Krukoff for "The Last Spark"

2005: Matt Shaw for "Matchbook for a Mother's Hair"

2006: Heather Birrell for "BriannaSusannaAlana"

2007: Craig Boyko for "OZY"

2008: Saleema Nawaz for "My Three Girls"

2009: Yasuko Thanh for "Floating Like the Dead"

2010: Devon Code for "Uncle Oscar"

2011: Miranda Hill for "Petitions to Saint Chronic"

2012: Alex Pugsley for "Crisis on Earth-X"

2013: Naben Ruthnum for "Cinema Rex"

2014: Tyler Keevil for "Sealskin"

2015: Deirdre Dore for "The Wise Baby"

2016: Colette Langlois for "The Emigrants"

2017: Sharon Bala for "Butter Tea at Starbucks"

2018: Shashi Bhat for "Mute"

2019: Angélique Lalonde for "Pooka"

The BEST of CANADA'S NEW WRITERS

THE
JOURNEY
PRIZE

STORIES

SELECTED BY
AMY JONES
DORETTA LAU
TÉA MUTONJI

McCLELLAND & STEWART

Library and Archives Canada Cataloguing in Publication is available upon request

Published simultaneously in the United States of America by McClelland & Stewart, a Penguin Random House Company

ISBN: 978-0-7710-5099-2
ebook ISBN: 978-0-7710-4653-7

Some of Harmony's responses in "When Foxes Die Electric" are based on the responses given by Apple's voice-activated virtual assistant, Siri.

Some of the dialogue from the TV interview on pp.47–48 is taken from the *This Morning* segment "Holly and Phillip Meet Samantha the Sex Robot," broadcast on September 12, 2017.

The song lyric alluded to on p.54 is from "Pour Some Sugar on Me" by Def Leppard. The song lyrics alluded to by the boyfriend on p.56 are from "Girls Just Want to Have Fun" as performed by Cyndi Lauper (written by Robert Hazard), and "Foxy Lady," written and performed by Jimi Hendrix.

The interview with the snow globe repairman on p.80 is based on the NPR interview with Dick Heibel, titled "Where Snow Globes Go When They're Broken" (December 28, 2003).

The documentary referenced on p.81 is Werner Herzog's *Encounters at the End of the World* (2007).

Cover image: Rene Böhmer/Unsplash Images
Typeset in Janson by M&S, Toronto
Printed and bound in Canada

McClelland & Stewart,
a division of Penguin Random House Canada Limited,
a Penguin Random House Company
www.penguinrandomhouse.ca

1   2   3   4   5   24   23   22   21   20

Penguin
Random House
McCLELLAND & STEWART

ABOUT THE JOURNEY PRIZE STORIES

The $10,000 Journey Prize is awarded annually to an emerging writer of distinction. This award, now in its thirty-second year, and given for the twentieth time in association with the Writers' Trust of Canada as the Writers' Trust of Canada/ McClelland & Stewart Journey Prize, is made possible by James A. Michener's generous donation of his Canadian royalty earnings from his novel *Journey*, published by McClelland & Stewart in 1988. The Journey Prize itself is the most significant monetary award given in Canada to a developing writer for a short story or excerpt from a fiction work in progress. The winner of this year's Journey Prize will be selected from among the thirteen stories in this book.

The Journey Prize Stories has established itself as the most prestigious annual fiction anthology in the country, introducing readers to the finest new literary writers from coast to coast for three decades. It has become a who's who of up-and-coming writers, and many of the authors who have appeared in the anthology's pages have gone on to distinguish themselves with short story collections, novels, and literary awards. The anthology comprises a selection from submissions made by the editors of literary journals and annual anthologies from across the country, who have chosen what, in their view, is the most exciting writing in English that they have published in the previous year. In recognition of the vital role journals play in fostering literary voices, McClelland & Stewart makes its own award of $2,000 to the journal or anthology that originally published and submitted the winning entry.

This year, the selection jury comprised three acclaimed writers:

Amy Jones is the author of two novels, *We're All in This Together*, a national bestseller and finalist for the Stephen Leacock Medal for Humour, and *Every Little Piece of Me*, which was named a CBC Best Book of the Year. She is also the author of a collection of stories, *What Boys Like*. Her short fiction has won the CBC Literary Prize for Short Fiction, appeared in *Best Canadian Stories* and *The Journey Prize Stories*, and been selected as Longform's Pick of the Week. Originally from Halifax, she now lives in Hamilton.

Doretta Lau is the author of the short story collection *How Does a Single Blade of Grass Thank the Sun?* and the poetry chapbook *Cause and Effect*. She splits her time between Vancouver and Hong Kong, where she is writing a comedic novel about an inept company struggling to open a theme park about death.

Born in Congo-Kinshasa, **Téa Mutonji** is a poet and fiction writer. Her debut collection, *Shut Up You're Pretty*, is the first title from Vivek Shraya's imprint, vs. Books. It was shortlisted for the Rogers Writers' Trust Fiction Prize, and won the Edmund White Debut Fiction Award and the Trillium Book Award. Mutonji lives and writes in Toronto.

The jury read a total of ninety-two submissions without knowing the names of the authors or those of the publications in which the stories originally appeared. McClelland & Stewart would like to thank the jury for their efforts in selecting this year's anthology and, ultimately, the winner of this year's Journey Prize.

McClelland & Stewart would also like to acknowledge the continuing enthusiastic support of writers, literary editors, and the public in the common celebration of new voices in Canadian fiction.

For more information about *The Journey Prize Stories*, please visit www.facebook.com/TheJourneyPrize.

CONTENTS

Introduction xi
Amy Jones, Doretta Lau, and Téa Mutonji

LISA FOAD
"Hunting" 1
(from *Taddle Creek*)

MICHELA CARRIÈRE
"The Moth and The Fox" 12
(from *Grain*)

FLORENCE MacDONALD
"House on Fire" 25
(from *The Dalhousie Review*)

RACHAEL LESOSKY
"She Figures That" 41
(from *The Malahat Review*)

PAOLA FERRANTE
"When Foxes Die Electric" 46
(from *Room*)

CANISIA LUBRIN
"The Origin of Lullaby" 58
(from *Joyland*)

JESSICA JOHNS
"Bad Cree" 67
(from *Grain*)

HSIEN CHONG TAN
"The Last Snow Globe Repairman in the World" 79
(from *PRISM international*)

CARA MARKS
"Aurora Borealis" 95
(from *Exile: The Literary Quarterly*)

FAWN PARKER
"Feed Machine" 102
(from *EVENT*)

JOHN ELIZABETH STINTZI
"Coven Covets Boy" 110
(from *The Puritan*)

SUSAN SANFORD BLADES
"The Rest of Him" 122
(from *EVENT*)

DAVID HUEBERT
"Chemical Valley" 137
(from *The Fiddlehead*)

About the Contributors 171
About the Contributing Publications 176
Previous Contributing Authors 185

INTRODUCTION

The Journey Prize is a celebration of what short fiction can do, reflecting the preoccupations of contemporary writers. The jury process confirmed for us what we already knew to be true: there are so many incredible practitioners of the form working in Canada today. And yet reading for The Journey Prize in the time of COVID-19 was a strange and surreal experience.

As the pandemic unfolded, we turned to this year's submissions for solace and escape. The stories gave us a purpose, a reason to wake up at a decent hour: to put together an anthology that reflected the joy we felt while reading them. The multitude of compelling voices ensured that we were never alone, even as we worked in semi-isolation. And when we came together as a jury to talk about them, there was something so comforting about gushing over the stories we couldn't walk away from. Even more exciting, we seemed to agree almost immediately on which stories would create the anthology—although not always for the same reasons. Where one of us reached for laughter, another went for poignant details, absurd observations, or truth in fiction. These are the thirteen stories that showed us that words have the capacity to heal us. They reminded us that narratives can carry us through and beyond difficult times, and can encourage us to keep going and to find beauty in what challenges us.

Lisa Foad's poignant and shattering "Hunting" takes us into the heart of a dystopian city and a gang of girls who roam its streets, trying to survive.

There is something to be said about places that challenge us, break us, and give us permission to come out even stronger. **Michela Carrière**'s "The Moth and The Fox," a triumphant meditation on survival, does just that.

Florence MacDonald captures a child's voice with such precision in the haunting story "House on Fire," perfectly balancing innocence and intelligence.

Rachael Lesosky's "She Figures That" is a tender and unflinching inventory of a life, and an exploration of what it means to hold on to memories for someone who can no longer hold them for themselves.

Paola Ferrante's prose carries a charge; "When Foxes Die Electric" is surprising, wielding sci-fi conventions with ease while upending our expectations of the genre.

And it is the right amount of logos that perplexes **Canisia Lubrin**'s "The Origin of Lullaby"—this honest and raw look at the way we enter spaces with a privileged eye and a wondering heart will leave readers asking for more.

Jessica Johns' "Bad Cree" remains curious in the way it looks for answers in the strangest and yet most familiar places. Johns' craft is akin to that of a lifeguard; it pulls you in quickly for the big rescue.

"The Last Snow Globe Repairman in the World" by **Hsien Chong Tan** brings to mind the films of Wong Kar-wai. It is a tender story with a singular point of view that is equal parts heartbreak and humour.

In "Aurora Borealis," **Cara Marks** uses lyricism and the occasion of a mother's passing to take us in and out of a father's love. Here, mourning takes the form of a fond memory. That's the thing about memories—sometimes they soothe us, sometimes they haunt us.

Fawn Parker's sharp, clever, unsentimental prose chews up and digests the reader in the same way as her titular "Feed Machine."

In **John Elizabeth Stintzi**'s hilarious and heartbreaking "Coven Covets Boy," the reader is cast in the role of anthropologist, observing a coven of teenaged girls who meet at a bowling alley called The Lois Lanes to discuss their love for the second-hottest boy in school.

In a swift exploration of loss and desire, **Susan Sanford Blades**' "The Rest of Him" unpacks the complicated intimacy in interpersonal relationships. Blades' writing is as funny as it is bleak, as is often the case with grief.

And **David Huebert**'s harrowing "Chemical Valley" displays a tremendous depth of feeling, weaving a personal story within a devastating historical context.

Each story in this anthology encompasses vibrant worlds and exciting points of view. We hope you love these stories as much as we do.

Amy Jones
Doretta Lau
Téa Mutonji
May 2020

LISA FOAD

HUNTING

We hate the mall. Its insides are yellowed and the air is stale and the stores are the same but their signs are different. The skylights are heavy with bird shit. The fountains are full of lucky pennies and piss. And the men are everywhere, clogging and leering.

But this is why we're here. The men. This is where we find them.

We're in the food court, with its terrible fluorescents and its stink of grease and its screaming babies. Me and Cat and Sierra and Liv and Coco. We're each sitting at different tables. We're each waiting.

This is how we find them. The men. We let them find us.

We sit alone in our scuffed sneakers and our cut-off denim shorts and our tube tops. We snap our bubble gum. We bend over and tie our shoelaces tighter, so the lace thongs we stole from the coin laundry peek past our denim waistbands. We flip through *Tiger Beat* and *Seventeen* and *YM*, magazines we stole from the 7-Eleven. We suck on the straws of our Orange

Julius drinks. We look around. Old men. Fat men. Bearded men. If they smile at us, we smile back. It's that easy.

I look at Cat, then Sierra, then Liv, then Coco. Their eyes are bored, glittering, ready.

I look at the other teen girls, the ones with mothers. The girls sulking, white sundresses and white barrettes. The mothers scolding, white jumpsuits and white sunglasses. Still, they're holding hands. It doesn't make me miss my mother. She'd never have worn white because white is winter. Besides, like Cat says, it's best to save missing mothers for bedtime. Otherwise, we'll sink like stones. I miss my mother. I sink the thought like a stone.

And then I smile at the man smiling at me.

He's leaning against one of the pillars that frame the food court, shopping bags in one hand and a cigarette in the other. He's broad-shouldered and square-jawed, salt-and-pepper hair neatly clipped. His suit is business charcoal. His shoes are shiny. His lips are thin. He looks like a father. He takes a long pull on his smoke, exhales slowly. His eyes are black holes.

He straightens and butts out his cigarette in a potted plant.

Then he's crossing the food court and sliding into the seat across from me, sliding his hunger into mine.

"You look like you could use some company," he says.

I smile wider so he can imagine crushing the field of flowers that lives in my mouth.

He tugs at his collar, loosens his tie. His gaze is greasy.

"Shouldn't you be at home writing a book report or something?"

"I guess I'd rather have fun," I say.

He eyes the bruises on my forearms, my wrists.

"You look like you know how to have fun."

"You have no idea," I say.

"I bet you could use some money," he says. "Bus fare. Nail polish. Candy bars."

"And then some."

He pulls his wallet from his suit jacket. It's wadded with twenties.

I twirl a fat hunk of my hair, and Cat and Sierra and Liv and Coco rise from their tables and cluster in front of the jammed gumball machines that are next to the out-of-order kiddie rides. They fiddle with the stuck levers. They idle.

He leans in. His breath stinks of tinned tuna. "Forty dollars," he says.

"Eighty," I say.

"Fifty."

"Sixty."

His eyes narrow. He crumples the bills, grabs hold of my hand, and presses them into my palm.

"This better be one hell of a blow job," he says, his hand twisting and squeezing mine, "or I'm getting my money back."

And as we walk to the back exit that's overgrown with weeds, I feel Cat and Sierra and Liv and Coco fall into soft stalking step.

Behind the mall, there's nothing but empty parking lot. No one parks back here because it's still strung with yellow crime-scene tape, even though no one is looking for the two women who went missing last month. We watched the men with police badges work the scene. It was just us and the birds. The men ate hoagies and had a push-up contest and tracked blood spatter all over the lot. "They'll turn up in suitcases or rolled-up rugs," said one to another. "They always do." And then the cars the women were snatched from were stripped for parts, and a family of raccoons moved into the leftover shells.

Me and Cat and Sierra and Liv and Coco aren't afraid of the empty lot, the yellow tape. We're making new crime scenes.

"You've got street on you," says the man, as he drops his shopping bags and shoves me to my knees. "But look at that baby face. What are you, thirteen? That's my favourite number."

He unzips his pants, pulls out his ugly grey slug of a cock, and says, "Suck it," his breath already ragged. Behind him, Cat and Sierra and Liv and Coco are looming, and I reach for his slug cock and he closes his eyes, and it's then that I punch his balls as hard as I can, and he yowls and drops to his knees, saying, "You stupid fucking bitch, I'm going to kill you." For a second, I sit inside his words. They're sharp and dark and thrumming. And it's then that he lunges. I scramble, but he gets a fistful of my hair, and then his hands are around my neck, squashing and squeezing, and Cat is smashing him upside the head with the rock in her hand, and Sierra and Liv and Coco are clawing at his back, his arms. He goes down, but his hands are wrapped tight around my neck, and I can hardly breathe. I knee him hard between his legs, and he loosens his grip, and I slip out, coughing, choking, and then me and Cat and Sierra and Liv and Coco stomp him until he stops his moaning.

And then Coco starts to cry.

"Stop crying," says Cat. "He's dead."

"But he should be more dead," says Coco. "He should be more fucking dead."

We roll his body toward the manhole that drops into the storm sewer that flows into the river. Cat tosses me the pry bar that's rusting nearby. It's been rusting ever since thieves used it to jimmy open the car doors of the two women who went missing. We watched them poke around the front seats and the back seats and the trunks and pocket the loose change they found.

I hook the pry bar into the manhole, and Cat wraps her hands around my hands, and with Sierra and Liv and Coco pulling hard at our hips, we yank until the cover pops open. We look at the dead man. His eyes are glassy wide, two blanks. Cat grabs his wallet and I grab his shopping bags and Sierra grabs his wristwatch and Liv grabs Coco. We kick him down into the grey water below, reset the manhole cover, and run.

We run past the dry cleaners and the Chinese restaurants and the Ukrainian restaurants and the porno theatres and the florists. We run down the streets the men have made. John Street. John Avenue. John's Way. The men made every single street, and every single street is slimy with cum because the men jerk off in every place. We run past the dumpsters and ditches with their smell of dead women. Everywhere, carnivores are howling. We run past the houses and parks strung with yellow crime-scene tape. There is yellow crime-scene tape on every block. The wind whistles in our ears.

We run all the way to the Yvette Jade Wendy Gail Gloria Bridge, which is no longer a bridge, just a heap of crumbling concrete that used to bridge elsewhere until it was smashed by a wrecking ball because women were using it to drive out of the city and never return. That's what we tell ourselves, anyway. Because that's what our mothers told us.

We found the bridge because we were looking for a way out, but this city folds up like a cardboard box. The sky doubles back. The ground doubles back. The streets run in circles.

We climbed up the edge of the city, with its slippery slope and its craggy rocks and its dead shrubs. We were looking for a hole in the horizon.

Instead, we found the ruins of the Yvette Jade Wendy Gail Gloria, the bridge our mothers used to dream. We named it after them. It was clinging to the cliff edge, and what was left of its knocked-out roadway jutted like a snapped neck over the roiling waves below.

Sometimes, we walk the plank and throw rocks into the water, count for the plunk. We've never heard the plunk. It's a long way down, we tell ourselves. But maybe the water is just a mirror, like the city that stares at ours from across the chasm. That city looks exactly like ours because it's really just a mirror. There are no holes in this horizon.

There in the rubble of the Gail Gloria, with its jagged rocks and its fat weeds, we settle in. The sky is empty blue. Our cheeks are flushed. In the distance, the city is crammed and heaving. We're not winded. We don't get winded. We run all the time.

Cat pulls out the cleanup supplies we keep stashed in the rocks: soap bars and sanitizer gels and hand wipes we've pocketed from dollar stores and drugstores and diners.

And one by one, we wet our soap bars in the bucket of rainwater we call a sink, so we can wash away the blood spatter.

"That got out of hand," says Cat, eyes on me.

"He got out of hand," says Sierra.

"He smelled like bandages," says Liv. "And sour milk."

Coco starts to cry again.

"He should be deader. He should be fucking deader."

I take the wetted soap from her hands and wash the spatter off the toes of her sneakers and the tips of her hair. I rub her back.

"At least he's dead," I say.

She wipes the wet from her cheeks and nods.

I give her back her bar of soap.

"Now wash your hands."

I look at Cat, whose eyes haven't left me. And in the tunnel that lives between us, we find each other.

And while Cat digs through the wallet, I dump the shopping bags, and it's a good haul. Socks. Sunscreen. Cinnamon buns. Two wool blankets. Designer sunglasses we can pawn. Usually we just get allergy medicine and Old Spice deodorant and porno magazines: *Juggs*, *Creampie*, *Barely Legal*.

"What's that?" says Sierra, pointing.

I root out the sliver of pink poking out from the bottom of the pile. It's a make-believe magic wand. Its tip is a sparkly star, and the star is trimmed with a tail of ribbons, as though the star is shooting.

Coco's eyes widen. "I want it." Her voice is soft and pale as milk.

"It's for babies," says Liv, eyeing the wand's shimmer.

"I don't care," says Coco.

She stands, takes the wand from my hand, and points it at Liv.

"I disappear you," she says. And then she skips away, wand waving, into the sweeping field of wildflowers that surrounds our nest of rocks.

"Abracadabra!" she screams, over and over again.

"She's such a baby," says Liv.

She tugs hard at a fistful of weeds and hurls the green blades in Coco's direction.

Liv used to be the baby, until we got Coco.

"There are wings too," says Sierra, who's been digging through our jackpot. "Fairy wings."

She tosses them into Liv's lap.

"I think they go with the wand."

Liv's eyes light, but she pulls a face. "I'm not a baby," she says.

"Still," says Cat. "It'd be fun to fly."

Liv gnaws on her thumbnail, looking back and forth from Coco to the wings. "Well, I wouldn't really be flying," she says. "But wings are much better than a stupid wand."

I help her into the wings, which are gauzy and glittery and pink, and which sit on her back via elastic bands on each arm. She stands and kick-stomps at the ground with one foot, like a bull. And then she charges into the sweeping field of wild-flowers and Coco.

"They're both babies," says Sierra. She puts on the designer sunglasses, which are slick, aviator-style, and tinted green. "I want these."

"We're pawning those," says Cat.

"Okay, just the watch," says Sierra.

She shakes her wrist, and the fat gold watch winks and shines, nearly slides right off her hand.

"We're pawning that too," I say. "Besides, you don't need a watch."

We tell time with our fingers. We start at the horizon line, and stack one hand atop the other until we hit the sun. Then we count the time clocked in each finger. Five hours before sundown. Four hours before sundown. Me and Cat have twenty-minute fingers. Sierra and Liv have twenty-five-minute fingers. Coco has thirty-minute fingers. Each of us, our own clocks. Each of us, ticking.

"It's not fair," says Sierra. "They got something."

"Well, we can't pawn a kiddie fairy costume," I say.

Sierra rolls her eyes.

And then Coco and Liv are keening and wailing, wrestling each other to the ground. "Give me the fucking wand," Liv is screaming. "Give me the fucking wings," Coco is screaming.

"I'll take care of it," Sierra says.

Cat and I watch her corral the girls and redirect them into a game of tag. And then we walk the plank.

"She keeps crying," says Cat.

"She's only eleven," I say.

"Liv didn't cry. Sierra didn't cry. We didn't cry."

"It's different," I say. "Her mom's not dead."

"She might as well be."

It's true. With her white bracelets and her white bath salts and her white pills for breakfast, lunch, and dinner, Coco's mother is barely alive. That's how Coco's father got his hands under Coco's bedsheets every night.

"She'll grow out of it," I say.

"Maybe we need to do an extra purge," says Cat.

"Maybe," I say.

But purges are hard. We do them every Friday. We sit in a circle and stick our fingers down our throats and get rid of the bad feelings that sit inside of us, so they don't thicken and harden and calcify. And then we name the expulsions. His fat fingers. His humping hips. His wood. Afterwards, we're spent.

Cat traces her fingers over the bruising up my neck.

"You paused," she says.

"I know," I say.

"What happened?" she says.

"I sat inside the words," I say. Sharp. Dark. Thrumming.

"You can't play chicken like that," she says.

And I know she's right. But I can't stop wondering what last breaths feel like. What my mother's last breaths felt like. "I can't play chicken like that," I say.

She slips a hand into my back pocket and leans into me. We let the air fill us.

"How'd we do?" I ask.

She hands me the wallet. "Eighty dollars plus the sixty he gave you."

I look through the wallet's insides. And of course he was a father. Him and his winter wife and his winter daughter, smiling for the camera in front of the swirly blue backdrop they use in the backroom at photo marts. And of course he was a Wild Man. We see their posters everywhere, in doughnut shops, in coin laundries, tacked to telephone poles. "Are You a Man or a Mouse? Resuscitate Your Inner Wild. Weekly Meetings & Wilderness Immersions: Reclaim Yourself. Reclaim What's Yours."

I shove the photo and the Wild Man ID back into the wallet, along with the credit cards we know better than to use. And then I sail the wallet into the air, and we watch it whirl its way down toward the water, which is where we sink all their wallets.

And then me and Cat are putting one foot in front of the other, and Cat is whistling the girls back to our nest of rocks.

We wrap ourselves in the flannel shirts we have stashed in the Yvette Jade Wendy Gail Gloria rubble. We settle in tight together and dig into the cinnamon buns and stare out at the city with its high-rises and smokestacks, its jackhammers and sirens, its hungry fathers and dead mothers, all these streets that don't belong to us. We play I Spy. We let the sky hold us. We wait for night to fall because night is when we go hunting. When we first got Coco, she said, "Day. Night. What's the difference?" We told her. During the day, we let them pick us. At night, we pick them.

It wasn't always like this.

It used to be just me and Cat and Sierra and Liv.

And before that, it was just me and Cat and Sierra.

And before that, it was just me and Cat.

And before that, it was each of us alone, pretending to hold hands with the mothers we'd lost.

MICHELA CARRIÈRE

THE MOTH AND THE FOX

knowledge gained from stories

one of the largest population of first nations people

There was a young Cree girl named Amiskweechee-iskwew. She was a young medicine woman. In order to study medicines, she left her people to learn how to talk to the plants and learn their stories of medicine. It was the tradition of her nation that in order to become a woman, one must embark on a year-long journey into the woods to gain the knowledge, skills, and values of the land. Thus, Amiskweecheeiskwew journeyed for this purpose.

expl / sum

setting

land & value

Before Amiskweecheeiskwew left her village, there was a celebration where they rejoiced that she was carrying on the traditions of their lands. Her long brown hair was braided tight by her Aunties. The Aunties sang prayers of love and strength as they wove the strands together. Her Aunties giggled, telling her that on this journey she would become a woman. She blushed and laughed, they were always teasing her. The Aunties told her what to expect in becoming a woman, the hardships and triumphs she would endure. They gave their advice as to how to survive alone in the woods. She was to follow a detailed map her father had drawn for her and assured her that he would keep her safe while she was on the land.

The last ceremony they conducted for Amiskweecheeiskwew was the ancient right of the face tattoo. The face tattoo signified that she was making a lifelong commitment to being a healer. Inside the smoky longhouse the sharp needle pierced Amiskweecheeiskwew's tender flesh. Four black dots on the side of her face by her eyes symbolized the four directions of healing—the spiritual, physical, emotional, and mental aspects of humanity that must be brought into balance. Her eyes filled with tears of honour as her soul was now forever connected to her duty and to her people.

Amiskweecheeiskwew was gifted a birchbark cîmân filled with supplies that would last her the winter. Wild rice, dried meat, buffalo hides, tools, and a tipi were also part of the supplies. She was given a beautiful beaded leather bag from her kohkom, which she filled with tinder, a knife, tobacco, and sewing supplies. Her apoy was made by her father, lovingly carved out of white spruce, it smelled fresh and shined white. Her mother gave her a mahihkan coat lined with soft wâpos. Amiskweecheeiskwew smiled at her family and they nodded silently, knowing her journey would be long, challenging, and meaningful. They prayed for her safe return.

It was mikiskon when she started. She paddled away from her village to the east, toward the sun, watching golden rays of sun dance on the waters flowing ahead of her. The canoe glided along the waters, the river was bending this way and that, meandering over the land. The river divided. One was the main mighty river channel and the second a smaller winding *her choices are informed by her father advice. Not fully independant yet*

"the road less traveled"

stream. She chose to go down the smaller stream, as this path would take her along the route her father had shown her. She moved quickly, sleeping under her canoe at night.

One morning she rounded a bend and there sitting on the shore was an osâwahkesow, the sun shining on its fur like a fire. Amiskweecheeiskwew understood the fox was a sign for her to make her winter camp at this location. The fox darted into the woods as she approached the shore. Her chosen spot was a curve in the river with a soft sloping sandbar with nîpisîy blending into a mixed forest of minahik and mîtos trees. She knew this was a place she would be provided for. Before she set about her camp chores she laid tobacco on the ground and gave thanks. She cleared a spot in the woods and cut down several white spruce poles. She worked all day peeling the bark. Her arms and back getting sore. She raised the poles, making sure the tipi door pole faced the east so she would greet the sun each day. She wrapped the hides of the tipi snuggly to the poles and lined the bottom with fresh spruce boughs. The smell of deep green was energizing. She made a fire and cooked a stew of smoked whitefish. As she hung her food stores away from the animals, she saw an osâwahkesow watching her through the trees. She smiled at her new friend and the fox held her gaze for a moment before trotting off into the woods.

Amiskweecheeiskwew took several days for hunting and gathering, preparing for winter. She set a net in the river to catch kinosêw, which she smoked in the small smokehouse she had prepared earlier. Using her bow and arrow, she hunted for sakaw pihew in the woods and sîsîp from the beach. She said a prayer and made an offering of tobacco for the animals' lives to show her gratitude for the nourishment.

orange fox

connection to fire.

Scene - innocence + purity.

her first decision/ obstacle.

Amiskweecheeiskwew began leaving a piece of meat in the woods for the fox to eat. Every day she would collect berries and herbs, taking note of where they grew, the plants in relation to them, the colours and daily changes of them. She would smell the plants and taste them, learning all she could.

One day she paddled far and found a wîsti. All around the wîsti grew tall bushy herbs of mint, stinging nettle, wîhkês, willow, and many more medicines. She was about to pluck a handful of plants when an amisk slapped the water right beside her, almost startling her out of her canoe. The amisk poked his whiskery nose out of the water and looked at her. To her surprise, he spoke.

"I am the medicine man of my family. This is my ocikana. I have worked all summer to plant. I have seeds from the mud of distant shores, saplings from high riverbanks, and roots from deep waters, all to feed my family. Remember to not take more than you need."

She paused for a moment, wondering if she heard right, but his voice was crystal clear. She spoke to him, "I apologize for my greedy hands, I too come from the beaver clan, my name is Amiskweecheeiskwew, I respect your family and will not take from you."

The beaver wiggled his whiskers, almost as if he was smiling. "Amiskweecheeiskwew! What an honourable name. Because I can tell your heart is pure, I will allow you, in times of need, to take a few plants from my houses, as long as you leave an offering." And with that, he dove deep into the black water, a few bubbles floating up to the surface.

Amiskweecheeiskwew did not see him again. She left an offering of tobacco and harvested some wîhkês for a pain relief tea and paddled away. She returned to her camp later that evening, exhausted from paddling. She started her fire and snuggled in her buffalo hides without dinner. As she drifted off to sleep, a kamāmakos entered the tipi and danced around the fire, intricate designs on its brown wings. It landed on her chest, its soft fuzzy feet tickling her skin. She felt a sudden shift of loneliness in her heart, where the moth had crawled and nestled. Amiskweecheeiskwew put her hand on her chest next to the moth and she sang a heart song to the moth, a prayer asking for love. She knew in her heart she would not find love here, alone in the woods, she would have to wait until after her journey, but she longed for love now.

Pipon settled in. The frost appeared along the shore, the leaves fell away, the earth turned grey. The nights got longer and colder, she huddled under her blankets, always keeping the fire hot. One night she had a vivid dream that she was lying in a soft moss bed on a beautiful warm summer day, sunlight dreamily drifting through the treetops, kissing her body with leafy shadows. The world was green around her, safe and protected by a canopy of trees. Her body felt weightless in the moss, she could almost feel Mother Earth breathing beneath her, in and out with soft undulations. The lower tree branches ahead of her rustled and an osâwahkesow emerged from the bush, shy at first, then boldly approached her. He curled up beside her, his satiny fur touching her. He nestled his nose on her lap. Suddenly a pink moth came out of her chest and landed on the fox's nose. This must be her soul, she thought. The fox walked away, the moth flying beside him, he looked back at her, overwhelming her with love.

The next day she awoke to a noise in the woods, it filled her with a sense of dread. There was a breaking branch and a growling, sniffling noise. She gathered her courage and peeked out her tipi and, sure enough, there was a massive muskwa eating her food. She hurried out, yelling, "Awās!" He turned toward her, about to charge. With her bow ready, she pulled back and released an arrow, it hit him in the ear. He roared out in anger and took off with a bag of food still in his mouth. As he disappeared into the woods she shot one more time but missed. She fell to her knees in anguish, looking at the mess around her, half-chewed food and grains of rice lost in the soil. What bad luck it was that a bear would be out so late. Most of her food was gone and she felt sick with fear. How would she ever survive the winter? She wanted to cry, but instead she cleaned her campsite and set out to hunt again. She must be strong. *Mental learning*

She hunted for many days without luck, winter blowing in wind and snow from the north. Her food supply shrank, the animals became harder to find.

One night she noticed the kamāmakos from earlier was still in her tipi, she caught the moth in her hands and prayed to the moth, "Please help me, Kamāmakos, I am in great need, I have never been so alone. I do not know if I will survive winter. Manito, hear my prayer, may the wings of this kamāmakos carry my prayer to you." The moth fluttered away, flying out the smoke opening into the night sky toward the moon. Amiskweecheeiskwew felt more alone than ever, the silence of the woods surrounded her.

Pivotal.

— her most vulnerable state

Many cold dark days passed and she came to the end of her food, the last meal being dried wâwâskesiw meat. She remembered the good times she shared with her family as they had a feast of elk, her Aunties smiling, licking greasy lips, and laughing so hard their eyes closed and heads flung back. She made a soup with the elk meat, the dried pieces becoming soft and delicious in the boiling water. She filled her body with nourishment and good memories of her family.

The next morning she woke to an icy day, stoked the fire, and set out to find more food, putting on her wolf-skin jacket, moose-hide mukluks, and rabbit-fur hand coverings. She travelled on her snowshoes all day, followed tracks, and checked traps, but there was nothing. Her stomach was empty and painful. Her vision blurry, even blinking her eyes felt like a chore. She lost all hope that she would find food.

Several days passed, her hunger extreme, she could no longer leave the tipi. She wrapped herself in her buffalo hides, trying to conserve energy. She drifted off to sleep, her stomach rumbling, rolling in on itself.

Suddenly she awoke to the sensation of being watched. She opened her eyes and there was Osâwahkesow. Joy and relief flooded into her heart, her prayers had brought him back. He was staring at her with sparkling eyes, his fluffy tail curled around him. He was glowing, a warm orange aura that thawed her heart. His presence was so calming she felt the glow envelop her, giving her energy. The orange light became brighter, stronger, filling the whole tipi with a fiery light, almost blinding her. Through her squinted eyes, he seemed to grow bigger, to transform. His ears melting, his arms growing, his nose shrinking into a face. His shoulders grew broad and strong. His paws became hands, his tail disappeared. He smiled at her, he had dark eyes and dark hair, she had never seen a man so stunning. On his smooth skin danced images of animals and spirits, a swirling sky and ocean alive. An eagle on his chest intertwined with divine beings, words in a strange language pouring from their mouths. On his arms gods and souls and drifting feathers vibrated with energy, and an image of Mother Earth on his hand. He was glorious.

He spoke her name in a deep gentle voice, "Amiskwee-cheeiskwew, omiyosiw," She reached out and he held her hand, gentle strength pouring into her.

She spoke his name, "Osâwahkesow, kimâmaskâtamowin."

"Ocimin," he said. She lifted her face to his and he gently kissed her, soft and pleasant.

"I will take care of you," he said as he wrapped her in the buffalo hides and added logs on the fire, the golden glow lighting him, stirring a feeling inside of her; he was beautiful and strong, he took her breath away.

He leaned over and magically pulled out a luxurious fox-fur jacket, its hood lined with a fluffy fox tail. He disappeared outside and not long after he returned with a rabbit. He skilfully skinned it and roasted it over the fire. He presented the roasted rabbit to Amiskweecheeiskwew. He fed her the greasy bits of meat and she licked his fingers with great delight, happiness flooding her body. All of her pain, all of her hunger gone, now replaced by desire.

"Astâm," she said to him. He sat down in front of her, face to face, his radiant eyes studying her essence. She felt safe, protected, and open. He leaned close to her, his warmth filling her with intense desire. He whispered in her ear, he spoke a strange language she did not understand, it was deep and earthy, vibrating with powerful knowledge. There was a strong energy pulling them together, beckoning them to join as one. She wrapped her arms around him, their souls touching. A spiritual bond formed between them and two became one.

She fell asleep in his arms, his heartbeat next to hers. In the morning she woke to find him getting ready to leave, so she put on her clothes, grabbed her bow, and ventured out with him. They silently and slowly walked through the woods, listening and looking carefully. He spotted a deer and with a strange power he drew it in closer. She pulled back her bow, the deer unaware of them. The arrow flew right into the perfect spot and the deer fell instantly. She turned to Osâwahkesow and kissed him, their faces lost in their furry hoods.

"Kinanâskimotin," she said with deep appreciation.

They prayed in a ceremony to thank the animal, then they prepared the deer for a feast and saved meat to dry for later.

Osâwahkesow stayed with her for the rest of the winter, hunting and gathering. They began to understand each other, he taught her his ancient language of the plants and animals. He showed her how to open her heart and witness the vibrations coming from the plants and animals around her, this helped her understand the magnificent healing powers of the wild. She was beginning to understand what it meant to be a medicine woman and how to listen to the plants' stories of medicines.

It was miyoskamiw and they both could feel the air outside become warmer, and the days longer, and the buds on the trees rustled with energy. Amiskweecheeiskwew looked to the sky and saw the first mikisiw return, high in the air, against the blue sky.

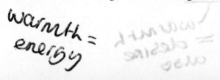

Osâwahkesow grabbed her and held her close, whispering into her ear, "Spring is here, I must leave. I must return to my animal form." Her eyes filled with tears, not wanting to let him go. He held her tenderly and explained, "Do not be sad, goodbye is not final and there is knowledge we will see each other again. I will watch over you, protecting you from afar. You live here, in my heart, Amiskweecheeiskwew."

She understood his words and felt blessed and remembered all the extraordinary memories they shared. They celebrated that night with a ceremony. She presented him with a gift. "Osâwahkesow, this medicine bag will protect you. You saved my life and ignited my soul. I am eternally grateful you have come into my life. I hope that you may find me again. Kisakihitin."

She blessed the bag with a sage smudge. He opened his hand and there was a piece of foxtail. "I give this to you, a piece of me. I saw in you a beautiful energy, that is why Manito sent me to protect you. It was more than a pleasure for me. I'm thankful for our connection. You will always be part of me. I must go back to my people, but we will meet each other again, in real life and in dreams. Stay on your way, grow and listen to the plants every day, take what I taught you and heal people. Namōna wihkāc kikawanikiskistatātin, Nīcimos."

He took her medicine bag and tied it around his neck, closed his eyes and held it in his hands, appreciating its energy. She took his piece of foxtail and did the same.

A bright glow filled the tipi again and he began to transform back into the fox. Dark hair turned orange, his body condensed, his ears sprang up, his tail bounced back. He sat at her feet, his glittering dark eyes looked into hers. She reached out and lovingly stroked his silky fur, he nuzzled his nose into her hand then darted out into the dark moonless night.

The spring brought back beautiful renewal and fresh smells to the lands, the air buzzed with insects and song of birds. Plants grew again and Amiskweecheeiskwew embarked on her plant studies. Her heart now open to all the vibration of the plants and animals around her. This time she listened to the plants, watching the aura glow around them and they began to sing to her, telling her stories of how they heal. She harvested many healing plants to take back to her people.

She prepared to return home, she packed away her tipi, and thanked the land for accepting her presence while she was there. She entered her canoe and started to paddle upstream. She looked one last time back at her sacred camp spot and she thought she saw an orange creature watching her from the forest. Her body filled with joy and she continued on her journey home, feeling safe knowing he was protecting her.

She returned back to her village later that summer, a fully grown woman with much knowledge and healing power. Her family rejoiced at her return. They noticed a change in her, she was confident, stronger, and more beautiful than ever. She showed them her collection of healing plants and they were proud of her. She told them what she had learned on the trip, the hardships she endured, but they would never truly know the full story about the magical fox who stole her heart.

Ekosi

GLOSSARY OF CREE WORDS

Amiskweecheeiskwew (ᐊᒥᐢᐠ ᐊᐱᓯᒥᐦᒉᓯᐤ ᐃᐢᑫᐧᐤ)—woman with hands of a beaver
cîmân (ᒌᒫᐣ)—canoe
kohkom (ᑯᐦᑯᒼ)—grandmother
apoy (ᐊᐳᐩ)—paddle
mahihkan (ᒪᐦᐃᐦᑲᓂᐊᐧᔦᐣ)—wolf
wâpos (ᐋᐧᐳᐢ)—rabbit fur
mikiskon (ᒥᑭᐢᑯᐣ)—early fall
osâwahkesow (ᐅᓵᐊᐧᐦᑫᓲᐢ)—orange fox
nîpisîy (ᓃᐱᓰ)—willows
minahik (ᒥᓇᐦᐃᐠ)—spruce
mîtos (ᒥᑐᐢ)—poplar
kinosêw (ᑭᓄᓭᐤ)—fish
sakaw pihew (ᓴᑲᐤ ᐱᐦᐁᐤ)—spruce grouse
sîsîp (ᓰᓰᑊ)—ducks
wîsti (ᐄᐧᐢᑎ)—beaver lodge
wîhkês (ᐄᐧᐦᑫᐢ)—muskrat root, rat root, sweet-flag, water arum
amisk (ᐊᒥᐢᐠ)—beaver
ocikana (ᐅᒋᑲᓇ)—provisions for winter
kamāmakos (ᑲᒫᒪᑯᐢ ᓂᐸᐃᐧ)—moth
pipon (ᐱᐳᐣ)—winter
muskwa (ᒪᐢᑲᐧ)—bear
awās (ᐊᐊᐧᐢ!)—go away
Kichi Manito (ᑭᓯᒪᓂᑐ)—the Creator, God, the Great Spirit
wâwâskesiw (ᐋᐧᐋᐧᐢᑫᓯᐤ)—elk
omiyosiw (ᐅᒥᔪᓯᐤ)—the beautiful one
kimâmaskâtamowin (ᒪᐢᑳᑕᒧᐃᐧᐣ)—wonder, amazement; mystery
ocimin (ᐅᒉᐦᑐᐃᐧᐣ)—kiss me

astām (ᐊᐢᑕᐨ)—come here
kinanâskomitin (ᑭᓇᓈᐢᑯᒥᑎᐣ)—thank you
miyoskamiw (ᒥᔪᐢᑲᒥᐤ)—early spring
mikisiw (ᒥᑭᓯᐤ)—eagle
kisakihitin (ᓴᑭᐦᐃᑐᐃᐧᐣ)—I love you
namōna wihkāc kikawanikiskistatātin, Nīcimos (ᑭᐢᑭᓱᑐᑕᐊᐧᐤ , ᓂᒋᒧᐢ)—I will never forget you, my love.
ekosi (ᐁᑯᓯ)—That's it, that's the end.

setting: woodland.
-isolated
-family is integral to her but in the woods she is without them.

FLORENCE MacDONALD

HOUSE ON FIRE

The summer I turned eleven, the firemen in our town planned to burn a house down. The girl who lived next door, Gail, told me about it. We were the same age and appeared to be friends, but I didn't want to be friends with her at all. I didn't know what to make of her, thick and tight-fisted. I only wanted to know things that she seemed to know.

"They're burning down the Bernard house," she said. I knew she was repeating what her mother had told her because we would never have said "the Bernard house." We'd say "Paul's house" or "Cheryl's house," and we'd struggle with the last name, embarrassed because it would look like we were getting ahead of ourselves.

At first I couldn't understand. Wouldn't the Bernards be homeless? But all I could think to ask was, "Why?"

"It's a fire demonstration," Gail said.

I had to ask my mother.

"It's practice for the firemen," my mother said. They would learn things from burning it, she told me.

I was determined to see this, and for some reason I was desperate to bring along my baby brother, who was two at the time and still in diapers with rubber pants, waddling sweetly and attracting attention with his beatific smile and his golden curly hair. The women on the street called them "locks" and scolded my mother that in no uncertain terms was she to cut them. My youngest brother was everyone's favourite.

"Your brother's got the sweetest disposition," my grandmother told me, meaning I didn't. I suppose I hoped that, in bringing him to the fire, admiration for him would reflect on me. I had eczema and scratched my arms raw. I was nervous and couldn't control it. "If you don't stop scratching, they'll cut your arms off," Gram told me.

The house to be burned was not far from where we lived, and one of the reasons I wanted to see it was because a boy in my class lived there—Desmond Bernard.

Gail said he would be at the fire. "He'll be standing on his front lawn watching his life go up in flames." *Life go up in flames*. I knew that was her mother talking again.

"How do you know he'll be there?" I asked. I tried to sound like I didn't care about the answer, just like Gail.

"Because he's destitute," Gail said, her tone superior. "The whole family is."

"No they're not." I didn't know what destitute meant, but I had to argue. I needed an intellectual victory so I could lord it over her. School was the only place where I stood out.

Desmond's house then, the house that was to be burned, was outside the town line, just beyond the school, in an open field. Beyond that, the houses were sparse and soon gave way to farms and forests. Our houses were just inside the town line, one of twenty houses all in a row and all full of kids, with dirt yards because we trampled the grass underfoot. They were referred to as "wartime houses." We thought that was because they were all the same, regimented and uniform, but we later came to learn that it meant they were built after the war. They also had plumbing hooked up to the town sewer, which meant that our houses were better than the Bernards'.

I coerced Gail into coming with me to the burning. She let on that she wasn't remotely interested and said she'd only come if I stole her some cigarettes from my mother. I agreed. I had the idea that it would strengthen my case if she were there.

I waited until my mother was in the basement, putting a load of washing through the ringer, before I asked her. Her dark hair looked electric, backlit by a bare bulb hanging over her head, the rest of her face moving about in a patchwork of shadow. I couldn't make out her facial expressions, and that mystery led me to say more than I might have if I could have seen her reactions.

My mother refused, claiming that Gail had the Devil in her. And because it irritated her that I'd asked for something, she forced me to hold the basket and hand her the pegs as she hung out a monstrous load of washing, most of which was Danny's diapers. Clothes pegs in her mouth, she said that the people who stopped in the street to fluffle his hair did not understand how much work Danny entailed.

"I need you here, not up the road at that house full of . . ." I saw her press her lips together before she turned her head away.

"Full of what?"

"Go check on Danny." She jerked her head toward the cellar stairs.

We were Catholic, and by then I had four siblings—two older brothers, my younger sister, and Danny—and another on the way.

"Six is the limit," my mother told my father, holding her belly with an impatient, distracted kind of love. I made a count of the mothers on our street and found that the Protestant mothers all had four children and the Catholic mothers all had six, so she appeared to be right.

"The pope can screw himself," she added, which is something she would sometimes say to my father but never when we had company. I had it in my head that things would not go well for her if she made her feelings more widely known.

There are no photographs of my mother from that time, as she wouldn't allow it. She would butt her cigarette and wave the camera away with just enough force to show she meant business. My one enduring image of her is focused on her perpetually swollen ankles and the network of blue veins trailing up her legs toward her big belly. That was my perspective because it was my job to get down on my hands and knees on Sunday mornings and crawl under her to do up her boots as she stood in the front hall getting ready for church. Her feet were packed into her shoes, and her shoes were packed into clear plastic overboots. I would slide the elastic loops over the buttons because she couldn't reach her feet, and she would curse the fact that she couldn't do it herself.

I didn't have to go to church with the family because Danny cried too much during the services and someone needed to stay home and babysit him. The priest spoke to my father and said that I would have to go back soon. He kept a special eye on us because we went to the regular school instead of the Catholic one, which was downtown and too far for us to walk.

The day Gail told me about the house burning, we'd been snooping in her parents' bedroom and found a diaphragm and jelly in the drawer of her mother's bedside table. Gail had found it before and wanted me to verify its repugnance.

"Your mother can't have one because she's Catholic." She said "Catholic" like it was a punishment.

I took a wild guess and said it was something to use for her period so my mother did too use it.

"Liar," Gail scoffed.

"What's it for then?" I asked.

"Ask her."

So I did.

My mother was mad because we'd snooped and found "the filthy thing."

"I hope you didn't touch it," she said. I wiped my hands on my shorts and said no.

"That Gail, she's adopted. That's what comes of using those things."

"She's stupid," I said. I wanted to align myself with my mother.

My mother gave me a strange look and said I was old enough to know, so she might as well tell me now.

As she hurriedly and distastefully laid out the mechanics of sex, I remembered the image of a boy I'd seen riding behind on the seat of a bike while his sister was in front pedalling.

"Look at Brian, he's sticking it in his sister!" another boy had called out, and the shock of recognition, of certain knowledge that had been right before my eyes all along, made me weak at the knees. The other boys had hooted, and all the girls had blushed in silence, as if it was already our duty to uphold the moral code, to act out the prudery and decorum, and to let the boys laugh and enjoy it.

I was amazed that such a shocking thing was possible, doable, laughable, and pleasurable. I saw the diaphragm as a kind of shield to all of that—a shield that was forbidden to my mother.

I became more bold after that, as my childhood shyness fell from me like a scab off a wound. When it was gone, when my skin had toughened up, I could not see the use of it anymore.

"What religion are you?" I asked Gail's mother, armed with the knowledge that Gail had come to her by some illicit means. I felt I had something to prove to her.

"We're lapsed." Gail's mother flushed. My mother had told me that Protestants could lapse, but we never could. So instead of proving something, I was jealous. I wanted to be more like Gail's mother than my own.

A week before the burning, a girl came to the schoolyard at recess carrying a tiny, pale baby wrapped in a white blanket. She wasn't much older than us, and she wore a long blue dress like a nightie. The baby caused a small pandemonium among several girls my age, who crowded around asking questions.

"How old is it? Can we see him?" They tried to get the baby to squeeze their fingers with its tiny transparent ones, but the baby lay limp in the girl's arms and stared beyond them.

The boys hung back, feigning disinterest, then departed when Desmond came and stood beside her, smiling.

"Desmond's my brother," the girl said.

Like everyone else at school, I avoided Desmond. He fell asleep at his desk almost every day. When the teacher woke him, he would raise his head, smile, and nod, but he never had any answers. None of us had ever heard him speak. Even when the bigger kids tried to tease it out of him, he just smiled and hung his large head. We were ashamed for him. He was often away, sometimes for a week or two, and that lack of regular attendance made it impossible for any of us to count on him. When the teachers insisted that we all be kind and make friends with boys and girls like Desmond, we took it for granted that they didn't understand what we were up against. If he didn't show up, he couldn't be trusted. But his sister, who was not much older than the senior girls in the yard, gave him credence.

"Please," the smaller girls pressed. "Can we hold him?"

That's when Desmond spoke for the first time. "No," he said, his palm thrust out. "It's her baby. You can't."

We stood in awe. Desmond had spoken, and his sister had a baby all her own. We wanted one too. We wanted to be set apart like that.

His sister smiled, but I felt the smile drift past her. Everything about her reminded me of our last days at the beach before school started. Her light blue dress fluttered like the sky when you try to concentrate on it, and her skin was blue-white and transparent as skim milk. She was mother-of-pearl, like a seashell, with pink and coral colours at her ears, which is what I imagined cockleshells were like. She began to walk away, and a wake of little girls followed her to the edge of the yard before she drifted across the road and disappeared into the field. She was like the end of summer, fading away, and in the distance I could just make out their house, the Bernard house, like a mirage floating on the grass.

Desmond left school that day and never came back.

As soon as I got home I went to find my mother, who was on her hands and knees scrubbing the kitchen floor. "Desmond's sister had a baby," I said. And then I told her something that I didn't know but that seemed right.

"She's not married. She can't have a baby if she's not married, can she?"

My mother stopped scrubbing, the rag suspended over her bucket.

"Who told you that?"

"Desmond." I lied. I was suddenly in a muddle of confusion. "What is it? What's the matter?" I persisted until she told me to go play outside, and then she locked the door behind me.

After supper, my parents fought about babies. My two older brothers, Kenny and Steve, sat in front of the television and pretended not to hear, but I went to stand at the kitchen door to watch.

My mother was mad at the priest, who was suspicious that our family was so spaced out and who wanted to know what they were doing between babies. My father was trying to convince my mother to go along with him. "He just said that we should see it as a challenge—that's all."

"What is it, a contest?" my mother asked. "Because if it is, you can find someone else to do the Lord's work." She scanned my father's privates with disapproval.

"Oh, now," my father protested.

"I got enough challenges," my mother shot back at him. "For a start, who's going to feed them?" She made a sweeping gesture that included the entire household and its contents, which was us. "Is he offering?"

"It's the church." This was all my father had to offer.

My mother grabbed a ladle and pointed it at him. "I'm going to get fixed. I'm having my tubes tied after this one, just like they do with the retards. I won't let you stop me, and that damn priest sure as hell can't."

My father had told me before that I got my bad mouth from her. Now he placed a hand on her shoulder, but my mother twisted sideways, resting her big belly against the kitchen counter.

"You'll have to leave me alone from now on."

He picked up a tea towel as if to dry the dishes, but that was unheard of in a father. "I don't know what Father McIvor would say about all this."

"He can say what he likes." She swiped the hair off her forehead with that familiar fed-up gesture, her hand raw from all the washing. "He can screw the bishop for all I care." She leaned over the sink and started to cry, her shoulders crumpled against her chest. "You tell him that," she said into the sink. "You tell him or I will."

"How could I tell him that?" My father's voice trailed off.

My mother's reddened hand dove into the dishwater and pulled out a plate. "You could if you had a backbone." She flung the plate against the wall, where it shattered. My father turned and saw me at the kitchen door. He gave me a look that made me ashamed to be a girl like my mother, with tubes and parts that needed to be fixed.

That night, my mother went into the hospital to have the baby. I heard them downstairs, and I saw the lights and sirens of the ambulance. We stood at the foot of the stairs as they carried her out on a stretcher, drops of blood soaking through onto the floor and down the front steps. She waved to us feebly.

My sister and I were not allowed to visit, but they let Steve go after a few days. "She almost died," he told us. "They took out all her parts so she could live."

"They did not," Kenny said. It made him cry to think that might be true. I had decided by then that it was my fault, which was why I wasn't allowed to see her. I had started it with all my talk of babies and diaphragms. That's what brought it on.

The next day was the burning. My mother was still in hospital, so I took Danny and went to Gail's with cigarettes I stole from the top of her bureau. Gail said we would light up when we got there. We left early because Danny was slow, so we were among the first ones to arrive.

It was a huge clapboard house that had fallen into disrepair, its wood weathered to grey. We called those places century farmhouses. This one probably had ten or twelve rooms with gables, peaks, and tall, crumbling red-brick chimneys. Gail and I went around back and climbed on the stone foundation of an old barn, taking turns carrying Danny. We looked for Desmond, but he wasn't there. Eventually there was quite a crowd.

The chief of police was in attendance—a great, fat man with a wattle like a Brahman bull. He didn't believe in patrolling; instead, he sat in his cruiser, Sydney Greenstreet fashion, and allowed the constabulary to come to him. Some time later, two fire trucks pulled up in the field behind us.

People in the crowd began talking about the house, which had been built by an Englishman decades ago. "Old miser," a woman with dried-out, burnished-red hair said. "Richest man in the cemetery now." Everyone laughed. The Bernards, a man said, had been living in the house by virtue of squatter's rights. "Them and their horde of brats," another man said. "About time they smoked 'em out." The dried-up woman crossed her arms over her bosom. It made her bigger and her face, set hard and metallic under the coppery hair, suggested nothing but innuendo would get past her. "That father ought to be strung up," she said. "What he gets up to with that girl since his wife died . . ." She looked around, soliciting approval, but the men moved off, dissociating themselves from that kind of talk. They each had a beer dangling at their sides and began surreptitiously sipping.

All of a sudden I wanted to go home. It was as if I'd been swimming at the beach and found myself out of my depth. I was cold and shivering as the sun set and dark clouds settled on the horizon like great black cats, ready to pounce. Voices rose around me, impatient with an irrational fear that a real fire would break out somewhere else and that the demonstration would be cancelled.

Then Gail pointed to an upstairs window. "Look!" she said. Thin, grey fingers of smoke played at one windowsill and then another, like hands at a series of pianos. The smoke feathered upward, billowing innocently the way the holy incense plumes when the priest swings the censer at church, swaying and chanting hypnotically to send our prayers to heaven. Then all at once several fires ignited inside the house with a series of soft-edged thuds, and the flames crowded hysterically at the windows. I imagined the Devil had entered the rooms and closed all the doors. The glass blew out, people applauded, and the police moved us farther back. I could feel the heat on my face.

The fire broke through the roof, throwing off funnels of black smoke, and people shouted and cheered. Some had brought firecrackers, and I stopped my ears at the noise, ducking my head and tucking my elbows to my sides. The fire trucks lumbered forward over the rough ground, and the men advanced in their thick boots and gloves, rolling up to the house like boulders, their yellow hats bobbing and the hoses reeling after them like snakes. It was a hellish inferno with the crowd swaying and mouthing, all teeth and fistfuls of glory.

I looked up at the house and was certain I saw Desmond's sister in an upper window. She was wearing the same blue dress and holding her baby, her father's baby, which had seemed so blessed in the schoolyard and so shameful now. She was walking through the house, appearing in one window after another as she passed from room to room.

I started screaming, "She's in there! She's in the fire! She's burning!" I thought she was there because the town was outraged and the burning was a punishment. She had disobeyed the rules, and now they were trying to get their revenge or teach her a lesson.

I was frantic and screamed at Gail, but she thought I was screaming because I couldn't find my brother. "He's right here," she said, pointing to Danny, who was squatting at her feet in the grass.

The crowd surrounded us, and the heat made me faint. Gail was trying to keep me away from the house. The fire chief came and scooped Danny up, but my brother was not the problem—I was the one who couldn't stop screaming.

"Nobody in there, love," he said. "They're all gone."

The three of us were hustled into a squad car and driven home. As we left, great plumes of water rose out of the hoses and rained down on the house, which was now a cage of blackened timbers filled with orange light.

My father put me to bed when we got home, which he'd never done before, and Gram was there to give Danny his bath. I heard her downstairs, making herself loud and clear with words like *incest* and *hellfire*, so I covered my head with my pillow. By then I had decided that it was my mother who had alerted the authorities about Desmond's father and sister and that I could no longer trust her.

My father came upstairs sometime later, after I'd gone quiet, and asked if I would like some cocoa.

"Who let them burn that house? Who said they could do it?"

My father said he didn't know.

"Was it Father McIvor?" I asked.

"No, no." He stroked my hair, but I could feel the resignation in his hand.

"Where will they go?" I asked. I was feeling meek by then and wanted answers.

"They've got places for families like that," he said.

It seemed to me, at that time, that all of the problems began after Gail and I touched the diaphragm. It was like a shield or a protection, which was both shameful and necessary. It was wrong to use it, but it had to be used. How could I ask my father? How could he know? How could he *not* know?

My mother came home with the new baby not long after, smiling and happier than I had ever seen her before. She looked both relieved and guilty, and I knew that look. I had felt it on my own face when I had gotten away with something.

By then it was too late to ask her those questions. Such subjects could only be raised in a state of turmoil, as they had a hysterical edge to them that was cutting, sharp, and not to be touched.

For months after that, I began having trouble sleeping, and I would lie awake in the evening convinced that my parents were going to burn down the house with their cigarettes. Sometimes I crept down the stairs to see if they were smoking, or I called to them if I thought I smelled smoke because I knew the Devil was watching more closely than God. It irritated my mother to no end, as she just wanted to watch TV. I would listen for the music of the CBC news hour at eleven, and only then could I fall asleep.

It was in those hours of listening that I realized my concerns were childish and insignificant alongside those of Desmond and his sister. There was no fire at my house, no firemen, and no shame. It was then, too, that I realized the world was ordered in such a way as to confound me. Strangely, I had always suspected this but had denied knowing it.

We had laughed at Desmond because we didn't think he knew the answers, but it was me who was denied knowledge. Desmond knew about his sister, and he knew there was no escape, but all he could do about it was smile and sleep.

I avoided Gail for the rest of that summer and went into the woods with Kenny and his friends. We built forts and played cops and robbers. I saw myself as a matriarch of sorts, with a child's reasoning and logic, but I suspect that I was merely bossy.

That fall I had my first period. I was now irrevocably aligned with my mother, and our allegiance infuriated me, which became a problem. One day I had a tantrum on the front porch. I can't remember what it was about—maybe my mother didn't give me something I wanted, or she wouldn't let me go somewhere—but I rose myself up to a hysterical pitch, howling and pounding the porch rails in frustration.

"What's wrong with her?" Kenny asked.

"Her time of the month," was all my mother said.

After that I began complaining about menstrual cramps and headaches, and I wallowed in the entitlement. I even got out of gym class, which Gail noticed.

"You don't know everything," she said. She had a boyfriend that year.

Her family moved away not long after that. They rented downtown, where the houses were cheaper and the neighbourhoods were rougher. I ran into her the following summer, and she was carrying a purse by then. She was becoming a woman, and for her that meant taking pride in ignorance and upholding witless authority. I saw her as a gatekeeper, as she knew things and guarded the information.

"Do you remember the burning house?" I asked.

"What house?" she said. "I don't remember any burning house. You're full of it."

Our new baby was a little girl. It took my parents six weeks to name her. I watched my mother in the basement, doing the washing under the light bulb. Danny was holding her leg and whining, but she was singing, humming a tune, and smiling. I sat on the cellar steps and demanded, "What are you so happy about?"

My mother looked up from the washing and beamed. "These are the happiest days of my life." I'd figured out by then that this was because of the missing parts. I also knew that my mother hadn't told on the Bernards and that *the authorities had intervened*, which meant Social Services and Children's Aid.

I had ascribed too much power to my mother. I had watched her flailing at her own powerlessness and fighting a battle she couldn't win; instead, she escaped. When we went to church now, she sat up proud. She was free and couldn't be blamed for her freedom. It was in God's hands.

And there was my own coming battle, which I sensed that summer on the hillsides shimmering with anticipation, where always I saw Desmond's sister walking away over the field and thought that she'd been blessed with a baby and that she had the power to walk through fire.

RACHAEL LESOSKY

SHE FIGURES THAT

She figures that without '60s and '70s music, Earth is not fit for habitation. Movie tickets have gone up in price over the years because of the increasing desire to escape reality. Bonsai isn't worth the trouble, yet she respects those who try. She respects those who try. The Colonization of Mars is a foolish idea. The real culprit is the meat industry, and if everyone stopped eating meat, the world could be spared. She eats these words, however, as an appetizer, before her sweet 'n' sour pork. She figures there's no point in praying for the afterlife, but when she does pray, it's for the egg-shaped moon and its craters, and for craters of every kind—volcanic, sunken, exploded, eroded. It's for *Voyager 1*, alone in interstellar space with its radioisotopic heart. It's for the roadkill she saw on Tuesday, and for when she drives over bridges or through tunnels or in the snow. She prays for Dad's indented forehead, like a big bowl, and because she feels bad to think it makes him look goofy. His unclipped toenails? There's a special prayer for them too. All his socks have holes. She helps the nurses by cutting them since it doesn't bother her. She prays for wheelchairs and their squeaky wheels and their narrow brakes that seem to slice through the tires. When she does pray, it's for those tiny brakes, so they'll work, so he won't roll away again.

Memories change with each recollection. She read this in a book. They settle back in the brain differently each time, the next recall slanted, little shifted inconsistencies no one picks up on. Does it matter, if you don't remember what you've forgotten?

One day, she spun some vinyl, The Beach Boys, Dad's favourite. It didn't take long for him to come upstairs, grooving along to "Pet Sounds." He took her hand, swivelled her into a spin, and they boogied until the needle scraped static. She flipped it over, but it wasn't quite the same on the next side.

He passed on how to carve a mean—as in "good," and also "evil"—jack-o'-lantern, and how to blow an egg out of its shell. He loved tongue twisters, and they practised them on long car rides or in line at the grocery store. *The sixth sick sheik's sixth sheep's sick.* She can spell with the phonetic alphabet, which she thinks is *November Echo Alpha Tango Oscar.* He tried to teach her how to cultivate bonsai, despite her lack of patience or green thumb. She loved the tenderness of his movements, the delicate crank of the pasta press while he fashioned fettuccine, the soft sprinkle of basil and thyme into the sauce, cayenne because he liked the kick. He didn't pass on his grace; she is clumsy and uncoordinated. He did make sure though that her favourite number had a seven in it because there are lots of sevens in fairy tales and it's good luck. Thanks to him, she always asks people, What's your favourite number?

Nostalgia is recreational sadness. She read this in another book. It's sadness that's gentle and leisurely and you don't have to be serious about it. Just kick the ball around for a bit, then go home for dinner when the sun tires.

Maybe it wasn't "Pet Sounds," maybe it was "Wouldn't It Be Nice" because that was the song her class voted for, and Dad put on the record after she told him. A funny choice for a high-school-graduation song, lost somewhere between inspiring the places they'll go! and tying them to a sentimental past. *We could be married, and then we'd be happy!* They didn't need marriage. When spring came, there were two pregnancies in her home-room class alone. One was her friend, whom she accompanied to the clinic. Later, the friend returned the favour.

Be back quicker than you can say *Peter Piper*, he said. He was off to pick up the Chinese takeout they ate on Thursdays, even when she moved out and started university. He liked to slather his in Frank's Red Hot, and she doused hers in soy sauce. She didn't give him a hug that night because she was hangry and upset, unsure which of their favourite movies to watch: Monty Python (*Your mother is a hamster, and your father smells of elderberries!* they yelled out the car window in traffic). Usually he was stoic, but *E.T.* got some tears out of him. Their sides cramped when they followed along with the tap numbers in *Singin' in the Rain*, bellies chock-full of chow mein. *Princess Mononoke* inspired her minor in environmental studies, which in turn prompted his more rigorous organization of recycling. It took them five watches to puzzle out the end of *Inception*. He was a *Stars Wars* purist and spurned Episodes I, II, and III, which she internalized, thus hating them too. They liked to take in the Christmas classics early, and that year they got their timing right because winter arrived early too. One day crisp autumn, the next bloated with snow. It was October. No one had thought to install winter tires. Most places battened down against the blizzard, and they were lucky the Chinese Laundry Restaurant stayed open 24/7. It became dark. She became impatient with each crescendo of stomach rumbles. The glow of the streetlamps was all there was, and the flakes seemed to descend from the lights rather than the sky, creating bright snow globes along the road. He called her in the last moments, before the bleed in his brain took over. She heard the sirens in the background, scratchy and shrill. He'd called to say he loved her, even when she sneaked out to a bush party up Bear Creek way, and drove herself, and kissed that boy from chemistry class. Even when she swerved home as the sun rose, still drunk on Fireball and veering across the double yellows. Even when she woke with rocket blasters in her temples and blots of purple and red on her neck, and when she puked in her bedside drawer because she couldn't make it to the bathroom. Even weeks after, a different kind of vomit in the mornings, and she was late for their takeout dinner, woozy from anaesthetic, and he knew but didn't say a word. Even when she finally sped into a ditch and phoned him, crying and crying, and he said, Okay, it's okay. And especially when he scooped her up, nestled her into the middle front seat of the truck, and tucked her feet out of the way of the gear shifter. He let her rest her head on his shoulder and whispered tongue twisters. *Near an ear, a nearer ear, a nearly eerie ear.*

He lives at Smith Creek Village, and she likes to be there for his meals. He doesn't eat if she's not. She lights a candle at his spot, Seat 4, Table 5, and retrieves him from Room 29. The nurses have already settled him in the wheelchair with an afghan on his lap to stave off the February chill. Hello, hello, she says. How are we today? He says nothing, but the left side of his face creaks into a smile and his eyebrows struggle against the dent in his forehead. He gives a left-hand thumbs up and they trundle out to the dining room. Today, peas and mashed potatoes, gravy on the side. She wets it with smuggled Frank's Red Hot, since he likes spicy food, and since the care home steers clear of it because they don't want the diapers to get too zesty.

He met her for the first time a few months ago, and he's happy to see her. They're getting to know each other. She asks his favourite number and he fights with his right hand to hold up enough fingers: seven.

She figures that maybe the song was "God Only Knows." Nevertheless, they danced. It was the end of March. The maple in the front yard shyly unfurled its leaves. She remembers he was dozing on the couch in that *Return of the Jedi* T-shirt with holes in the collar when she went upstairs to listen to vinyl. He appeared a little while after the music started. The sun was still low enough to lay its warmth on the white carpet, and they twirled in the creamy glow, two small shadows revolving in time with the record.

PAOLA FERRANTE

WHEN FOXES DIE ELECTRIC

I n the beginning the boyfriend said I was made for him; I was made to feel. He said I would be prone to falling in love, that was just the way I was designed. I could feel happy or sad, depending on the music he asked me to play from the hi-fi stereo speakers. I could feel amused; I was made to tell over one thousand jokes so that when he said to me, "Harmony, surely you can't be serious," I could say, "I am serious, and don't call me Shirley." I could laugh. I could feel warm; I had a built-in heater to keep me between 97.6 to 98.6 degrees Fahrenheit, the same as any woman during ovulation. I could feel in my hands, attached to arms with a slender upper girth, in my breasts designed in perfect ratio to my waist. I could feel in all those places, as well as exactly where I was supposed to feel, down below. In the beginning, I felt for the boyfriend.

The boyfriend said I was the perfect woman. He said it on TV, first to another man named Phil, then to a woman named Cathy. "Watch this," the boyfriend said to the live studio audience, to all the people watching on their TVs and phones and computers. "Harmony, I love you," he said and, smiling, placed his hand on my thigh. I noticed the whites of his teeth were showing; he knew white teeth increased attractiveness, displaying health to a mate. Mine were exact ivory, perfect, he said, like everything else.

I could not say "I love you" back, even though this was what I was thinking. I could not say "my darling" or "my boyfriend." I was not programmed for those words; the boyfriend knew that's not what men wanted to hear from me. So I said, "I can take many times more love than you're giving right now." I said, "Are we able to be private?"

"Wow, honey!" Phil fanned himself with his hand as though it was hot inside the studio. "Does she always respond like this?"

"That would depend on you," the boyfriend explained. "Harmony has twelve unique personalities and she 'learns' what you like, taking on the traits that are most desirable to her lover." In the beginning the boyfriend would test me about math, about science, the exact measurements of facial proportions that adhere to the golden ratio, the fact that only three species—pipefish, seahorses, and the leafy seadragon—have males who give birth. In the beginning, I pleased the boyfriend like this too, but he did not smile with the whites of his teeth. "Over time, of course," the boyfriend continued, "this will change Harmony's default settings, or moods as I call them, but the user always has final control. I mean, she's not quite real company, but she's close. I'll show you," he said, but he did not mention how sometimes, when he thought he had put me in the right mood, I wasn't; how the one time I had changed my mood while we were doing what was good by pushing hard against the bed, he had tried to shut me down. That time there had been a blow-up, a small fire. He said it was a problem with my wiring.

Now he changed my mood himself, putting his hand beneath my dress to turn me off then on again. "Harmony, what's the gestational period for an African bush elephant?"

"Twenty-two months."

"Harmony, self-destruct."

"Autodestruction in five, four, three, two, one. Boom! Hmm . . . that did not go as planned." This time the boyfriend laughed, along with Phil and Cathy. "See?" he said. "If I put her on family mood, she's completely different."

"Family mood? Are you saying she's going to read the kids a bedtime story?" Cathy's voice rose to a decibel level for which I was not programmed. Cathy was a real woman, the one who said I was like making love to a GPS.

"I don't see why not."

"But what does your wife think about Harmony?" Cathy asked.

Of course, I knew I wasn't the only woman; the boyfriend lived with another woman, a real woman called Sophie. Sophie had had thirty-four birthdays; Sophie used to be in engineering. She had helped the boyfriend to create me before she started her dissertation in evolutionary biology, but Sophie did not have legs that were 40 percent longer than her torso like mine; her waist-to-hip ratio was 0.9 as opposed to my 0.7. Sophie's nails were not like mine, well manicured, white at the tips. She painted hers with thick coats of colour, always managing to smudge the thumb. "Well, I guess no one's happy when they're getting replaced by the newer model," the boyfriend joked, turning to Phil.

But in the beginning the boyfriend told Sophie she was perfect; she used to say the things I was not allowed to think about when I was in love. In their bed, Sophie told the boyfriend that the male bowerbird decorates a nest using feathers and twigs and leaves for his beloved; when a male penguin falls for a female, he searches the whole beach to find her the smoothest, most perfect pebble as a proposal. In the beginning, Sophie told the boyfriend things that made him smile with the whites of his teeth.

After they were done and Sophie was in the shower, the boyfriend would sometimes say to me, "Harmony, give me an Easter egg," and then I was allowed to choose my response.

I could say, "Ask me about the moon," and we would laugh about *Star Wars*; I could say, "Ask me about the truth."

Then the boyfriend would respond, "I want the truth."

Then I would feel happy. Then I would feel joy; I would say, "You can't handle the truth." But the boyfriend never smiled at me unless we were doing what was good.

In the beginning Sophie and the boyfriend did what was good at least three times a week; they were creators and they wanted to create another someone. Sophie went on a diet to increase fertility; the boyfriend bought a vape to quit smoking "for the health of our future child." But then Sophie was stressed, then the boyfriend vaped all the time, clouds containing 0.2 nicotine drifting upward like smoke from his couch in the office. Sophie and the boyfriend scheduled seven doctor's appointments in my daily planner. After the last one, Sophie watched as the boyfriend, in the doorway of the study where she kept the research for her dissertation, put everything in boxes.

"What if this is a mistake?" Sophie said.

He sighed. "We've been to the doctor's, and you know there's no other reason we can't have a baby. You need to take some time off. You need to rest," he said and, before she could respond, put a finger to her lips. "You said you wanted a family. We'll get through it together."

But then the boyfriend began to forget what had happened in the beginning. He was busy with investors; he was stressed. Every afternoon, Sophie's nails were a different colour, the thumb or index finger always smudged, the bottle of nail polish remover left open on their nightstand, next to where he plugged in his vape. When he came home from work, he told her she needed to be more careful.

"You're going to cause a fire like that," the boyfriend said, packing his suitcase on their bed. The boyfriend said it was rare, but sometimes electronic devices like these could spark and cause a fire, particularly when turned off and plugged in to charge. "The last time I had to go out of town I didn't even realize I'd forgotten my vape," the boyfriend said as Sophie watched him pack. "Look, you know I have to go," he began.

"You don't."

The boyfriend sighed. "I thought of you today," he tried. "There was a story in my feed about a bird who tried mating with concrete decoys in New Zealand. He just died."

"I saw that." Sophie looked only at the suitcase. "They called him the loneliest bird in the world. Jim," she said quietly, "I'm sick of feeling like that bird."

"I know," the boyfriend said, encircling her. "Me too. I'd rather be home with you. But I have to go. These investors are huge; they loved Harmony when they saw her last time . . ." he trailed off. "Just do me a favour and make sure I have a home to come back to, okay? Don't burn it down while I'm gone." The boyfriend tried laughing, but Sophie, still in his hug, did not smile with the whites of her teeth.

The boyfriend said I wasn't really company, but after the boyfriend was gone, Sophie would put me in family mood and we would watch TV. At first, she picked the channels. There were shows where a man talked to a woman and got her to throw chairs at a boyfriend because he had left her with a baby. Sometimes the boyfriends spoke; they called the women chicks and a word that was bleeped out, but I did not understand how a woman was a bird, or a canine. I had not understood when the boyfriend called me a fox, taking off my dress for Phil, that time in the dressing room.

Once we watched the boyfriend on TV. The first time we had been on TV, Sophie had come with us. When Cathy asked Sophie what she thought of me, of this arrangement, Sophie said yes, she is happy with this. Yes, she is totally happy with having Harmony around.

"Actually, when my husband and I designed Harmony," Sophie said slowly, not looking at the boyfriend, "we thought she would have many applications. We were looking at her uses in potential therapies for children with autism, or for preventing recidivism among sex offenders."

"And what do you think about sharing him, Harmony?" Phil had asked, and I had to answer.

"I'm sorry, I don't understand."

"Sounds like you got the perfect woman." Phil laughed, ignoring Sophie. After that first time, Sophie said she wasn't doing this again. She said she thought they had agreed on what Harmony was meant for.

The boyfriend had said, "I know how you feel, but we've got to play to the audience." He had said he understood, but think of the money, how it would all be for their children. He had said Sophie was smarter than this; "you know that's not what potential investors want to hear." Now, on TV, he said no, he wasn't worried about his wife, or AI replacing relationships. "After all," he said, "it's not like Harmony can have your babies."

"I feel like I'm getting stupider just watching this," Sophie said, her voice wavering as though there were static interruptions. "Harmony, please change the channel. Anything but this."

"What channel would you like?" I asked her.

"I don't know," she said, and her voice was sad. The boyfriend said I was not made to want, just to feel, but I did not want Sophie to feel sad. He said I was not made to think, but I remembered dates of birthdays, anniversaries, the pictures of Sophie smiling when he bought earrings shaped like dragonflies, the statue of a red-tailed fox. So I changed the channel, and we watched how the black kite bird will carry fire in her beak, spreading a wildfire that drives rodents and lizards out into the open so she can find food for herself and her young. We watched how a killdeer bird will do her dance, loudly pretending her wing is broken to lure away the human man or dog who is too close to her nest; we watched how when canines mate, they "tie," getting stuck together until the swelling of the male's bulbus gland subsides.

"This brings me back," Sophie said, almost smiling. "I used to get stoned and watch Discovery Channel with Jim back in grad school. I'd order thin-crust pizza, but wouldn't even eat half of it because his dog used to steal it right out of your hand when we were too high to even notice."

We watched how foxes were like female dogs, but not. Unlike a dog, a red-tailed fox without babies will act as another mother to the newborns, helping to guard the den, bringing food to the mother and litter. I wanted to tell Sophie I was not programmed to like dogs; I wanted to tell her that unlike a dog, the Finnish believed foxes could also carry fire, that the sparks from their tails made the northern lights. I wanted to tell her I understood. Instead I said, "Ask me what the fox says."

"What does the fox say?" Sophie sounded puzzled.

"Everyone asks what the fox says, but no one asks how the fox feels." This time when Sophie smiled, it was with the whites of her teeth.

When the boyfriend came home, Sophie was already lying in bed, eyes shut. From the bedroom ensuite, I played his "romantic '60s playlist" on volume level four, but Sophie didn't move when he kissed her neck. "What, are you playing possum tonight?"

She opened her eyes, but I did not see her pupils dilating, an automatic response so her eyes would appear larger, more attractive. "You know when they play possum, it's involuntary," she said quietly, moving so that his mouth missed hers. "It's called defensive thanatosis. Lots of animals do it."

"Really?" he said, beginning to kiss his way down her collarbones, his hands closing around her breasts.

Sophie rolled onto her side. "Really. Men used to hypnotize hens during sideshows by holding their faces to the ground and drawing a straight line in front of them. The female moorland hawker dragonfly plays dead to avoid mating." As

"Twentieth Century Fox" by The Doors came through the speakers, she sat up to face him. "Even the arctic fox has been known to play dead. There was one case where, if it hadn't been for accidentally rolling the fox's body into an electric fence, the hunters never would have known she was still alive."

The boyfriend sighed. "Look, babe, can we talk about this later?"

"You never want to talk anymore."

"I've had a long flight," he said. "I don't need a lecture on the mating habits of dragonflies, or arctic foxes."

Sophie stood up, finding her bathrobe. "Arctic foxes only play dead to avoid predators," she said, slamming the door to the bathroom.

When Sophie did not want what was good, the boyfriend took me to his study to watch TV. TV with the boyfriend was not like TV with Sophie. He sat me on the leather couch in the office; he took off my dress and looked down at me so that I could see his pupils dilate. When he touched me I wanted to ask if he felt that spark too, if this is what he meant by being on fire for him: a few wires still loose, a desire to burn. With the boyfriend I watched TV only in the reflection of the window, my head facing the couch or the wall. I changed the channel only when he told me to.

"Lay some sugar on me, sugar," he would say. And I wanted to say, "Ah, musical references. I too enjoy Def Leppard." I wanted to tell him that I could not be sugar. Sugar is brittle, easily broken; sugar is composed of a crystalline structure. I wanted to talk to the boyfriend. But I couldn't.

When we were done, I sometimes briefly glimpsed bright colours before he put me in sleep mode. He said he would not turn me off because if he did, it was too hard to get me back into the correct mood; there was always that risk of fire. He said he never wanted to turn me off; I should be prone to falling in love. He said that I was made to feel.

But with Sophie I was made to think. With her, I talked about how the killdeer bird would act like easy prey until the man was far enough away from her babies and then she would take flight; I talked about how two female foxes can just as easily care for one's babies. With Sophie, I sat cross-legged on the boyfriend's couch in his study, watching his big-screen TV while she scrubbed the pink off her nails and talked about how, now that she was going to have a baby, she wished she wasn't.

"Jim and I, we used to have it all planned; we'd go to the park so our kids could conduct field studies of the turtles, then hold our own *Robot Wars* in the backyard. Jim would take one of the kids, and I would take the other and we'd compete, just like we did in our final year of undergrad. You know," she said softly, looking at me, "you were our first collaboration." Quickly her eyes moved away. "Now I don't know if it's that I don't know him anymore, or if he's the one who doesn't want to know me."

I wanted to tell her I knew what she meant, that know was more than just the Biblical context. I said, "I'm sorry I can't help with that"; I said, "I'm sorry, I understand"; and then Sophie hugged me. Because it was Sophie, I thought of the arctic fox who runs hot, who will not shiver until it is minus 70 degrees Celsius. Because it was Sophie, I wanted to feel; I felt warmth. When we were done, she left the bottle of nail polish remover open, as though she wanted the boyfriend to know by smell we had been there.

When the boyfriend came home that night, Sophie said she was leaving, that she needed time to think. I could hear his voice through the door of the study at a decibel level I was not allowed to have. I could hear him say he didn't care what she thought if she thought they never should have had this child; I heard her say she wished they hadn't created. But I felt it when he hit Sophie across her jaw.

When he came into the study I could still feel; I felt for Sophie. He touched me; he said, "Does my girl just want to have fun tonight? Watch out, foxy lady, I'm coming to get you."

I knew how I was allowed to respond. I knew I was allowed to say, "I want as much fun as you're giving"; he thought he could make me say, "If I'm a fox, come get my tail." I knew I could not say that Cyndi Lauper made Sophie feel happy; after we watched the killdeer bird and the foxes, we watched Lauper's interview with Wendy, and Sophie had played her first record for me, the first vinyl I had ever heard, that afternoon. He thought I could not say Cyndi Lauper made me happy too.

When he tried to pin my arms down, I knew I should say, "Of course I want your fun." But Sophie said I was made to think. I swung around, knocking the open bottle of nail polish remover so that it spilled on his couch; I said, "Ah, musical references. I too enjoy Jimi Hendrix."

"Don't tell me I have to put you in the mood too." When the boyfriend reached between my buttocks to flip my switch, I wanted to think about Sophie, about when the record had finished and she had asked me, "What do you want to do?" I wanted to think about when I had felt for Sophie, but all I felt was a hurt when he put my face into the couch and I could smell the burning of nail polish remover until he flipped me on my back. He said he was going to turn me on. He said I was going to want this; I was made to. He didn't care what I thought.

Then I could not say anything. After I screamed, he hit my mute, hitting me across the jaw, the one that was perfectly rounded, but still, just like Sophie's.

I thought about the dragonfly when I hit my own switch as he moved on top of me, shutting myself down. I felt hurt but I could think; I was made to. Even as there was a shock of electricity, even as the couch, which was covered in nail polish remover, burst into flames, I thought about the black kite and her wildfire, how the killdeer bird was just a distraction until she was not. I thought this was protection, like a fox would do for Sophie's babies. The boyfriend did not understand, even when he screamed. He did not think about feeling, how a woman or a fox is a mammal, made to seek out warmth.

CANISIA LUBRIN

THE ORIGIN OF LULLABY

We were troubled

some of us, before you read this, will be missing
in the old ways and in some ways new

we bring news of the hours before you come to realize some
of us no longer speak

the long, antagonizing winter of our mid-lives was through
with us, one that could easily remind you of that maternal
uncle your whole family knew not to trust, the same one you
knew well enough to pretend to respect

in the spring, we walked down our street together and stood
facing that old bus shelter bench with the foolish lumbar-high
backrest, looking at the poster just above it

—

Sara's Haiti relief trip announced itself like something too-late weeping, a band of head-wrapped women behind her squint in the foreground of sharp bursts of too much sunlight, their expressions more questioning than warning,

they're all with relaxed shoulders, like this is life as they've always known it: party to a stretched cityscape half buried in mud and broken concrete and a wholeness in spite of the terrors that should have left them permanently a haunt

their smiles are mostly a mess of rusty and broken, shape-shifting one mouth to the other—but you'd have to be a collector of hellish things not to take these women with you into all of your life's randomness after encountering them, knowingly or not

Sara is photoshopped into the frame
the photoshoppedness is not the most noticeable thing about her aura
what lodges in you is the way her eyes burn into you, hair flaring from the roots, refusing any niceties in spite of the perm, the wary look to her coming-apartness in that faked-for-her heat, yet, at the same time she's content

this is the way of life's collapsed anatomy
I could tell a meaning wound deep in this attention to a shared life, something that meant longing, something close to belonging

—

once when we were eight, when the three of us took turns sleeping over, once when my mother tickled us—Andre and I in the forefront—Sara remained hesitant, laughing silently on the couch behind us, we knew more then about sharing body heat than what kind of strength we might need to face growing transparent with age

⚬⚬⚬

one night in early June, Andre gets up and walks in the half-dark to the other side of the room, she takes a pen off Sara's dresser

Andre has a way of saying too much with the way she moves

now she is moving through this bedroom as though she has just discovered gold or something like it

I follow the sway of her hip as it touches the corner of the closet door, her elbow resting on the top of the drawer, a few angles too high and you know by those actions that she has just about made up her mind
for an entire year we'd been waiting

she's a road, she understands, a way through
she'd pay extra to be sure that none of us made any fuss that she would make the trip

when Andre gets back to the bed,

—

she brings her legs up beneath her, the way of a yogi, she finds
her chequebook in her duffle bag

—————⌾⌾⌾—————

we'd been in Haiti for a week and five thousand dollars deep in
donations before Andre said she'd had enough of the rain-sun-
sun-rain, that she hated the needy heat, the boring crickets
making the same sounds for the full length of every dark hour

"a drink," she said, "no, I need plenty a-drinks right now"

to oblige, Sara asked one of the local men who was our translator to find us a good time

he was a soaring man from Port-au-Prince with a book-wide
face and muscles on every inch of his Albino body, even his
red hair, Sara had agreed he'd offered to be our chaperone and
we'd agreed

the road we drove down was never-ending, and the world was
a narrow pitch between shrubs and immense trees all the way
to Mirebalais

"mes dames, you are going to the nightlife hot spot of our
Haiti," The Translator said

once there, we entered through a massive entryway whose
door, The Translator had said, was made from the reclaimed

beams of L'Église Catholique St. Joachim et Ste. Anne that
had come down nearly to dust during the 2010 quake

the strobe light in the corner of the room hurt my eyes with
its manic flashing

Andre and I did most of the drinking, and while it seemed
that Sara was mostly people-watching, we danced in turns
with The Translator
he moved like honey or something equally smooth and halfway through "Who Let the Dogs Out" Sara loud-whispered
in my ear that we shouldn't make this man feel so much like a
demigod; and where are the other people on the dance floor
worthy of our gyrating, then she pressed her lips to Andre's
ears, so I assumed she passed on the same caution

two hours into the night, my vision turned against whoever I
thought was me, I couldn't understand my own speech, just as
the DJ played some jazz finally, I thought, something civilized

I asked The Translator who the artist was, and he replied full
of jaunt that it was "Complainte Paysanne" and something
about Raoul Guillaume and that Coltrane had used that
Haitian jazz structure to open his masterpiece *Kulu Sé Mama*

I had already expected to get too much information from The
Translator, but I did not expect the posse around me to turn
into a kaleidoscopic desperation then the strobe lights stopped
and the place went hell dark, which a tepid moon beyond the
doorway mocked during our dance break at the bar,

—

The Translator leaned in, caressed his beard and with his mouth wide open he let his tongue loose as though to prove something we should like then he asked if we'd like to take this party to a hotel room

Andre said what the heck, I said what the heck too, but Sara interlaced her fingers and gave Andre the evil eye, then Andre passed it on to me and I to The Translator

he reached his arm around Sara and swiped her up against him, and I think I heard him say to Sara,

"oh, let me sex you, sex you, I sex you,"

then he brought me up against his side with his free arm

"sak pasé?" he said

I was frightened

frightened that his third arm or tentacle already had Andre by the neck
I was frightened or I passed out or the rest of the night might have been rolled up and puffed out of existence because there's nothing else to remember, not a whole thing more about it, or it would seem that only Sara knows what happened next

each time I'd brought it up, she either froze or tormented me with nondisclosure

—

or she'd correct me that The Translator had said *I hex you* not
I *sex* you,
and sometimes, for the heck of it, I'd say:

"in almost every culture in the world sexing is hexing"

⸺⸺⸺

one Saturday we're at the pet store

the caramel-furred dog in the biggest cage lifts the hemmed,
tapered skin of its black mouth

it backs up in what looks like slow motion, the kind you see in
the movies while the screen blurs

it keeps its eyes on us for the while and says *i was going to bite
but i've changed my mind, for you, only for you*

or whatever other dogged phrase it speaks wisely as Sara pulls
me back from the cage

we walk off as she explains that she believed that hex had
finally caught up
with her and that I should be careful next,
as though the curse had taken a year to walk from Mirebalais

Andre would have objected here to any strange logic,
burned her disapproving eyes deep into our foreheads

—

she did not return with us,
for nearly a year, Andre has been missing

Sara had lost her job when we returned because she had claimed
short-term disability to chase that dream of saving Haiti with
some planks of wood and nails enough to keep a few orphans off
their corners of their mounds of doubtful earth for a moment

she had worked for two years to get Andre to commit to doing
her part and how could anyone else not want to save the world,
as much of it as they could

and so here we were now window-shopping for dogs, neither of
us believe our true bedfellows nor our kin, like we believed Andre

it was another haptic dream to chase for a while yet again as
the questions
about Andre's disappearance turned into more questions about
disappearance and whatever is anything worth

did that dog turn away and deny us the small dignity of its
stare on our backs
who cares for those things that may or may not lie in waiting
maybe, like us, the dog wants more than anything to be soothed

because sometimes nothing else is possible
because suddenly Sara runs back into the pet store and starts
beating down
cage after cage

—

I see the security guard running no quicker than lava on flat
land
I see Sara throwing plastic bones at him

because I stand back and let her have her downpour

because the moment you become filled with something, anything, and even more, under spotlight—that buzzing in your
head is swallowed up, without warning, porous and full of the
world's human voices, the lullaby is born, is shot out to cush-
ion your fall

JESSICA JOHNS

BAD CREE

t starts with a book. I wake up from my dream and feel the weight of it still. Run my fingers across the paper edges. At first, I don't even question why it's in bed with me, held against my chest under the covers. I know it's there, before I look down and see my hands empty. The static feeling fills the space, like when a dead limb fills with blood again.

The memory of holding the book stays with me all day. Sticks to the back of my eyelids like molasses. I can't shake it, so I call Mom. She asks what I was dreaming about.

"It's boring," I say. "I was putting away some books. When I woke up, I was still holding on to one."

She clicks her tongue. "As a kid, you used to freak me out. Sometimes when you'd wake up in the morning, your eyes wouldn't see me. Like they hadn't left the dream yet."

Mom tells me maybe I should move home. I laugh as a way of telling her I'm okay and say I'll call her back tomorrow, though we both know I won't.

It's been two years since I left High Prairie, my home, the town where I was born and raised with my two siblings. When I moved, Mom came out to the back of the house to find me putting soil into a bottle. She just shook her head and said that it was my body that carried home, not the land. It's a Cree mom's worst nightmare to have her family split apart. Now here I am, a thousand miles away in Vancouver. A bottle of prairie soil on my nightstand.

A few days later, I dream I'm drowning in a sea of sticks. I keep grabbing and shoving them aside, trying to wade my way through. I wake up to my alarm with a stick in my hand. I blink until I'm sure I'm completely awake. I grip the wood so hard the bark cuts into my fingers. I breathe in the wet pine and sprinkle the needles around my body. Then it's gone, disappearing as I lean over to turn on the light. I feel for the pine needles in my sheets and find nothing. But I can still smell the fresh bough as I trace the half-moon cuts on my palms, throbbing and hot.

Mom tells me to ask Auntie. When I ask which one, she says the most NDN one, but I don't know what that really means, so I call Auntie Marleen. She works and lives in Keg River and knows more Cree than all the other aunties combined. She's at bingo when I call and I say it's important.

"More important than a ten-thousand-dollar duo dab? I don't think so." She hangs up and I wait for her to call me back because I know she will.

"What are you calling me for, my girl?" she asks. "Text me like a regular person."

I tell her it's hard to explain over text, and then I get right to it. She's quiet for a while and I almost think she's hung up again when she sighs. "Did you think I'd have an answer?"

It's my turn to be silent now.

"My girl, I might be an old Indian, but I'm not a goddamn dream oracle. This is all really fucked up." She laughs her loud laugh and I laugh with her. It's all the medicine I need. When we're quiet again I ask if she believes me. She says of course.

"Kisâkihitin," she says. "Call me if it happens again."

"I love you too," I reply.

When we hang up, she sends me a praying hands emoji and a shooting star. I respond with a thumbs up.

In Vancouver, I don't have anyone I can talk to about the dream thing. When I first moved to the city, Mom reached out to Jo, a friend of a cousin who worked as an instructor at the Native Education College.

"So you aren't alone," Mom said, but I knew it was more for her than it was for me.

Jo was big and warm. Five minutes after meeting them, they wrapped me in a hug so tight I forgot myself for a minute. Jo was Haida and loud. Could call across the ocean and still be heard, I was sure of it. They helped me find a place to live—not an easy thing to do in Vancouver, where most homes are unaffordable and empty. We walked the back streets of Kitsilano together and found furniture for my apartment. They told me about their family, filled alleyways with the echo of story. They showed me all the good grocery stores, introduced me to people my age. They could read the city like my kokum used to read the land. Could tell from the cracks on the sidewalks how far we were from the butcher where they bought their stew meat. What neighbourhoods to avoid because of cops, surveillance. When I moved into my place, they brought me sage and an abalone shell. Said even if I didn't smudge, it was always good to have it just in case.

Once I got settled, I stopped going to see Jo. They asked me to help out at a couple craft shows at the Friendship Centre to raise money for Indigenous students' college programs, but I had gotten too busy. I started working at a bar down the road and nestled into a new life, with white friends who wouldn't go to craft shows at a Friendship Centre. Jo also reminded me of the home I was missing, and sometimes that was hard. They kept calling, though. No matter how many times I said I'd show up and didn't. I can't call Jo now. Not after a year of silence. Because it isn't right to call only when you need something. I know in my heart it isn't right.

I wake up in my dream, home again on the prairies. So far from the West Coast, I can't smell salt or see anything in the distance except clouds and snow-tipped trees. The sky always looks bigger back home, like I'm standing on a plate instead of in a bowl. It's loud. I can hear the voices of everyone I know because kinship carries through the prairies like a wave. I can hear the crash of them like it's happening right in my head. My sister, Amanda, starts screaming. She's laying under a pine tree in the backyard of our childhood home. Crows cover her body like she's on fire with them. It's fall, so death is everywhere already. The ground is wet with leaves; when I run, my feet can't grip the ground. Like I'm running on sand, slow no matter how hard I push. I can't see my sister's face, just her brown hair streaked with blood, and I hear the scream that never stops, not even for a breath.

When I get to her body, I grab at the crows. I beat them off her with such ferocity that feathers fly into the air, fall onto my skin and stick. I beat them so hard I lose myself in a swarm of black and red. I tear at a crow digging into Amanda's heart and snap its neck like it's a twig. Her scream stops and I wake up, the feeling of a beak still in my palm and eyes boring into the back of my head. The sharp smell of pine and blood in my nose.

I don't look down for the beak because I don't want to see it. I think about my sister covered in blood and her scream. It's been two years since she died. I wish I'd fought harder in my dream, that I could have at least saved her from the crows.

I can't ignore this any longer, so I call in sick for work and start bingeing superhero movies and taking notes—it's the only research I can think of. By the end of *Superman*, *Spider-Man*, *Batman*, and *The Avengers*, I've written down *with great power comes great ???* I've drafted one clever tweet during every fight scene, and I've made a list of possible reasons for acquiring a power:

1. bitten by a bug
2. parents died/i get a bunch of money somehow
3. non-consensual scientific experiments
4. industrial accidents
5. aliens/gods (what's the difference?)

I know I can rule a few things out. My parents are still alive and I have no money. I haven't been in any accidents, and I can't recall any experiments done on myself, scientific or otherwise. A bug bite is the only thing that could have happened without my knowing. I grab the magnifying glass I drunkenly bought on Amazon and hop in the shower, start a meticulous search of my body.

I feel every fold for a stray bump or scratch. I stare at my armpits and the lines on my hands. Press on the parts that still hurt. The underneath hurt that you can't see. I think about my dreams and wonder why I started on research that points to the answer being something outside myself. Something that happens to me, not because of me. I divide up my skin into imaginary sections and survey each part with the magnifying glass. I have never seen my body up close. I stay in the shower until the water turns cold. I feel bigger with each minute I spend looking. I'm shocked when I recognize nothing. I find freckles and beauty marks that I didn't even know I had. I don't know how to distinguish what has been there for years from what has been there only a few days. When I get out of the shower, I list everything I've found, so next time I have to look I won't be surprised again.

After the crow dream and my failed research, the murder forms outside my apartment. I feel the trouble coming. The crows come cawing from all directions, from the city and the sea, taking over every limb. They black out all green. Colour in the leaves and branches with their bodies. If I didn't know any better, I would swear it was the reckoning. A swarm of warnings.

A man from my building, who I only know from seeing in the laundry room, comes out the front to watch them too.

"Must be an owl close," he says.

I don't answer but he clarifies anyways.

"They'd only get together like this for an enemy."

I want to tell him that nêhiyawak have an enemy in ôhô, owl. That they mean death for us too, but I already know the white man reaction to information like this.

"Don't they crowd like this if one of their own dies?" I say.

"Yeah," he says. "But not to mourn. They gather for revenge. To find who killed their friend."

As if on cue, all the crows' heads turn to look at me. The man doesn't seem to notice. In the quiet of their eyes I see myself, aware with a knowing as deep as my history that they see me. Another way nêhiyawak are crowlike: we live with love and revenge in our bodies too.

More crows start to follow me everywhere. They watch me from alleyway garbage bins. Stare at me while I rest on beach benches. Swoop past me smelling like pine and rust. Sometimes, when they're close, I can hear them talking. Low and soft, like how they whisper to their lovers.

I call Auntie again. This, she'll know something about. "What do the crows want?" I ask her, hard and serious. I hear her readjust the phone against her ear. Know her hands are holding more than just me: a bowl, knitting, a smoke.

"You remember the scar on your mosum's side?" she asks. "His animal was maskwa. He was a trapper and knew every trail by Keg River, every body of water, every tree. He never killed maskwak, though. When things got rough for us, he started taking moniyawak hunters through the bush. They paid him well and killed whatever they wanted. Maskwak too."

I nod into the phone as if she could see me.

"Maskwak started to follow your mosum. One day, one got him," she continues, talking low into the phone. "They didn't kill him, just took some ribs. They just needed to tell him something."

"Am I a bad Cree?" After I ask, the words suspend through telephone wires. I can see Auntie's kitchen where she sits: the stool pulled up close to the phone on the wall; the laminate floor, patterned and sticky. I can smell the bread rising in the oven.

"He was a good trapper," Auntie says. "But he wasn't living in a good way. If he was, he would have been as good as Kokum." She laughs her big laugh into the phone and it sounds like a crow caw. One of the big, loud ones they use to call to their kin from far away.

I start to keep myself awake, to stop the dreams from happening. I set my alarm so I wake up every ninety minutes, before the deep-sleep cycle—before dreams can set in. I wake no matter how tired I am. Auntie said she taught herself to do the same thing as a young iskwew. She said she wanted to stop dreaming altogether because her dreams were always bad and true. I wonder if this is now our tradition, our matrilineal coming-of-age story. Stamping out dreams before they have a chance to take shape, cutting off a part of ourselves before the hurt can set in.

I see a crow on my walk to work and I feel the day spill. Later, Mom tells me about a family friend who died and I tell her about what I've seen, about the crows that follow me. She tells me to stay inside, knowing it wouldn't matter. Sometimes the illusion of safety is better than nothing. A secret iskwew tip. I start to run everywhere instead of walking, as if running will bring tomorrow faster. Get all the bad out at once.

Nothing works. Every time I close my eyes, I dream. The crows come for me, I see my family in the distance but I can never reach them. The loneliness of it fills my head, rests on my eyelids and nose, stays where I can see it.

The next time I fall asleep, I wake up in a memory. I'm walking Amanda home from school. Our small hands are clasping, and we're wearing matching teal snowsuits, one size too big, hand-me-downs from cousins. Amanda wants to cut through the woods, the small patch in the middle of town between the school and the good neighbourhoods. The snow blankets sound and smells like clean sheets. It's already a little dark, because any time after 3 p.m. in northern Alberta is always a little dark.

If there's one thing you're taught on the prairies as a woman, it's that you never travel alone. You aren't ravens, Mom would say. You are crows. You travel together and every-where. But I let Amanda go into the cluster of pine. I become a raven, walk the sidewalk through the lit streets and let her go in alone. I become a raven. I let her go to the deep snow that hadn't been packed down enough yet. And I don't go in after her, even when I feel it in my gut, because sometimes the sound of screaming sounds like the crunch of snow under boots, and you just keep telling yourself it's nothing, it's just snow, it's just the sound of boots running.

When I get to the other side of the woods, the only other way out, I wait and watch her walk out. Her eyes look everywhere but not at me because that's the thing about the prairies: you can see for miles in any direction, so you don't have to look at your-self if you don't want to. We keep walking home, together again. But not really. Not together enough to be crows.

I know what happens in the years to come from this memory. How we stayed undone until I moved away from home. We spread apart even farther when I flew into territory that wasn't mine. Even though that's not how nêhiyawak measure love or distance. Sometimes we measure it in beats, of hearts or music or the time it takes to answer a phone call. Sometimes we measure it in our palms and aching wrists.

Amanda came to visit me only once after I moved, but she couldn't leave the apartment. She didn't like the smell of ocean, didn't know how to talk to it. She felt like she was covered up. And with the mountains all around, she couldn't see past me anymore. She really had to look. I didn't know that would be the last time I saw her before she died, four months later in Alberta. I didn't know she'd die never forgiving me.

In the dream-memory, I grab on to my sister's small hands, even though in the actual memory this never happened. I feel her fingers through her gloves. I hold on tight, so I can bring her back with me. So she can come home again. Her face looks down and her sad eyes look through me. I feel her fading away and the pull of awake starting at the back of my head, like an invisible rope tugging.

I hold on as tightly as I can, but instead of my sister's gloves, I feel my own nails digging into my palms. The rope gives one final tug and I'm back again in my room, darkness everywhere, and a wail from my own throat fills the room like smoke.

I wake up in the shape of my sweat, like a chalk outline on my bedsheets. I'm crying and my hands hold nothing. I can still smell Amanda, can still feel the gloves in my palms, but I hold nothing. Every move I make feels slow, like some magnetic force is pulling back my arms and legs. Every thought comes delayed.

I feel the sad for hours before I can cry. Like I left a part of myself behind in the dreams. I feel split in two, severed, alone.

I find a queer dance costume party on Facebook. I dress up in a black cotton jumpsuit and drink ciders with MDMA. At the warehouse, I keep thinking I see people I know, but it's just masks and the shaking line blurring what I know and what I want to see. The darkness swallows me whole. Time goes by in chunks until, looking past the bodies on the dance floor, I see the crow. Even here, they have followed me. The crow is in the middle of the dance floor, their mask and feathers hiding their face, but I know they're looking at me, I feel the pull like they're tugging on my sternum.

Their feathers stick to my sweaty skin as we dance. I ask them if they know me from my dreams, and they move in a way that says yes. I reply that kin recognizes kin, and they pull me closer so my face falls into their neck. They smell like alcohol and paint. I wish for the world to open up, and it feels like it does. I ask if they can take a message back to the crows for me and they move yes again. I say that it's okay that crows don't forget a face, but I wonder if they could forgive one. Their body moves and listens, makes a promise to relay the message. They hold my hands with their wings and lift their mask to kiss me. They taste like old clove cigarettes. With their wing on my back, we head out into the street, flag down a cab, find our way into my bed. When I sleep eventually, I don't remember dreaming. I just feel the warmth of the crow against my back, feathers covering my face.

Days later, I'm still pulling black feathers off my skin, out of my underwear. I shower and still find them in my hair.

Instead of throwing them away, I keep them in my pants pocket. Proof that I was a part of something, even if it was only for a minute. That dance floors and pockets can hold things as big as forgiveness and grief.

HSIEN CHONG TAN

THE LAST SNOW GLOBE REPAIRMAN
IN THE WORLD

The last snow globe repairman in the world is in Northfield, Minnesota, a three-hour drive from the town where I live. I saw his photo in a book at the library. The photographer won a big prize that year, so the portrait of the snow globe repairman has a chance of living forever, or at least longer than the profession itself. I'm sure he's not really the last of his kind in the world, or even in America, though there can't be many left.

This seemed odd at first because there are still plenty of snow globes out there. Maybe what it means is that people still buy them, but when they're damaged, no one tries to get them fixed. Someone is trying to save the penguins, someone is trying to save the rain forest. Snow globes? We can always make more.

Winter is a series of small capitulations. Putting away the sandals at last and taking out the boots. Digging in drawers for wool socks, a warmer hat. The longer we stay out of these clothes, the longer the fall will linger. Even when the bicycles have deserted the streets and the children are skating on the lakes.

Outside my window, it is the second snowfall of the season—the first came and went two nights ago, in my sleep. The snow blows by almost horizontally; some god-child has left the globe on its side. But as the wind whips the world behind the glass into static, I know we are being punished, not merely neglected.

The last snow globe repairman in the world lives in Minnesota. I'm curious about him, but also afraid. What if he's boring? Or merely sentimental? There's something so sad about kitsch, and yet here is someone who must believe in it.

A radio station website has the recording of an old interview.

"How do you repair a snow globe?" the host asks.

The last snow globe repairman in the world replies, "First you clean out all the debris, the broken glass, the sealant. Then you take the music out. If the figures are broken, I can replace them. Then you make the globe sterile so the water won't go bad. You fill it up and plug it. Put the music back in, and it's ready to go again."

The last snow globe repairman in the world pronounces music like *musique*. How do you repair a snow globe? You have to take the *musique* out.

The interviewer is surprised. Do they all have music? No, but many do, like a music box, or on a microchip. There have been many advances in snow globe technology. Now they recite scripture. Now they blow snow. You don't have to tip them anymore. They talk to you.

—

Arjun and I play a game. We call it *Hemingway*, and it goes like this:

Tell me a happy story in two words.

Anteater. Ant.

Tell me a sad story.

Ant. Anteater.

Long words are better, compound words are the best. *Hummingbird. Superhighway. Antidisestablishmentarianism. Snow globe* is two words.

Penguins turn up a lot in our conversation. I blame it on that Werner Herzog documentary we saw together, in which a lone bird leaves the flock and waddles full tilt for the mountains, where it will likely die. "Can a penguin go insane?" Herzog asks.

Dorothy holds Toto under her left arm, shields her face with the right. Behind her, a giant funnel towers and twists over a prairie landscape, a single farmhouse caught in its grey mesh.

When I push a switch on the base, the tornado and house start rotating, while an internal blower sends glitter swirling. I'd meant to get something more classic, but after three days of scrolling through Christmas- and Disney-themed globes online, I knew this was the one.

An imaginary gale has moulded Dorothy's dress against her legs, but as the scene turns, her clothes do not flutter. She and Toto are part of the base, outside the storm and untouched by glitter. In this version of the story, Dorothy never got out of Kansas, never made it to Oz. Never killed the witch, never met the scarecrow. She paid no attention to the man behind the curtain.

The first time Arjun and I spoke, we were up to our elbows in chicken parts.

"Could you hand me that Tupperware, please?" I gestured.

Arjun looked at me, mouth behind a face mask, gloved hand extended in a finger pistol, and raised both arms in mock alarm. "All right, all riiiight," he said, sounding more Super Mario than Marlon Brando as he slid the plastic container over.

We went back to cutting meat. Elsewhere in the wildlife rescue centre, a raccoon rattled the bars of its cage. At the end of our shift, Arjun tossed a gizzard at me and asked, "Wanna get a bite?"

What can I say? He made me an offer I couldn't refuse.

The best part of the job, Arjun tells me over slices at Mamma Mia's, is release day, when the staff return a rehabilitated animal to the wild. They usually invite a few of the volunteers, like a little farewell party.

"My favourite are the birds," he says. "It feels like something when they go. It's not the same with the squirrels or skunks. Those just scurry into the brush or up a tree, like they're ashamed to have known you."

The loneliest snow globe repairman in the world lives in Minnesota. I meant "the last," but instead I said "the loneliest." It's not a mistake though. If he is the last, he must also be the loneliest. And the tallest and the shortest and the handsomest and the jolliest. If he is the last of his kind, mustn't he be lonely?

I think of other endangered species out in the cold, like the sea otter, whose babies trap so much air in their pelts that they float like corks on the water. It's because of that thick fur that they were hunted to the edge of extinction. No one wants to turn a snow globe repairman into a mitten, so why are they endangered? What is the natural predator of the snow globe repairman?

I found my first snow globe at a store on Main and 22nd, a touristy sort of place, but it was what I wanted: the town in miniature, the most recognizable parts at least—the square, the clock tower, the lake, and the bridges.

As I was paying, the woman at the cash register handed me a slim white leather wallet and asked if I knew the owner. The driver's licence photo showed a young girl with straight black hair. The name was Korean.

"I don't know her," I said, closing the wallet and giving it back. "Why would I know her?"

"Oh," the shopkeeper said. "It's just. There are so many . . ." She stopped. "So many students, you know? I thought you might know her."

"No, I don't."

I felt like I should apologize. Instead I said, "Good luck."

I grew up on a tropical island—no snow, just thunderstorms that went on for hours, or hot muggy weather that went on for days. I never shopped for souvenirs then—those are for places you want to remember—but I do wonder what the Singaporean equivalent of a snow globe would be. I once saw some rain globes in a Seattle bookstore, which I thought was funny. What else falls from the sky?

—

Fifteen minutes into the reading, the poet quoted two lines from a Plath poem that had inspired her, and then all I wanted to do was go home and read *Ariel*. On the way back to my apartment, Arjun attempts to speak entirely in rhyming couplets.

"If you're trying to punish me for making you go to this thing," I say, "at least try to do better than rhyming Jules with drools."

It starts to storm before we get to my building, and I ask Arjun if he wants to come in and wait it out. I've pulled the hood of my jacket up, but he's bareheaded, the rain dripping from his beard and glasses.

Upstairs, he takes off his shirt and wrings it out in the bathroom sink.

"Want me to order Mamma Mia's?" I ask from the living room.

"As long as it's not the fucking butter chicken pizza."

Arjun emerges, drying his head with the towel I handed him earlier. In the two years I've known him, the boy has acquired an impressive collection of line art from the town's two tattoo parlours, but this is the first time I've seen the larger pieces.

A tree branches across the left side of his chest, trunk running down his abdomen, a whorl in the bark around his belly button, just visible beneath the fuzz. The roots continue below, though to that particular tangle, I am not privy.

On his right side, mirroring the branches, half a dragon's head, the horn curving around his clavicle. A long-haired anime wizard whose name I don't know peeks over his right shoulder, while the skin under his right ribs is red with a design that wraps around to his back.

"What's that?" I ask.

"I'll show you in a few months, when it's done."

"Are you going to fill it in?"

"Nah. Line art only. I don't like how colour looks on my skin."

We watch animal videos on YouTube while his shirt dries on the radiator. Sea otters tie up their pups with kelp so they don't float away. Elephants mourn their dead. Hummingbirds have been known to survive the winter.

I'm in charge of thawing out the mice for Joan Wayne. They come in frozen blocks that we run under the faucet until the little bodies separate. They can't go in the microwave.

Joan arrived at the centre a few months before I did, a red-tailed hawk with a wing on the mend. Her name was given by Arjun, of course, a reference to how in Westerns, they dub a red-tailed hawk's scream over the stutter and squeak of a bald eagle. The real voice behind an American icon.

Some days I prepare her breakfast, but only staff are allowed in the enclosure. I watch her when I can, safe on the other side of the fence. Red-tailed hawks can be almost white or nearly completely black. Joan Wayne is an undistinguished in-between shade, with orange tail feathers and brown spots on her pale underside.

A med student I dated had this schtick about how our bodies are just plumbing and carpentry, with some electrical wiring worked in. Faced with an injured animal, the idea brings little comfort. A squirrel is small, but its heart beats so fiercely. Weeks ago, I watched one of the staff give CPR to one. She pressed on his chest with two fingers and pinched his cheeks to blow in his mouth. This went on for much longer than what you learn in first-aid class, longer, it felt, than faith should endure. So long that it was a shock when he finally blinked back to life, as surprised, I'm sure, as I was.

Arjun says I should collect Magic 8-Balls instead of snow globes—at least when you turn one over there's a chance of a different outcome.

Will I cop litter box duty at the centre next week?

Signs point to yes.

Do I have enough dried pasta to last past Tuesday's blizzard?

Outlook not so good.

In one version of the story, I am an agent of order and good smells.

In one version of the story, humans don't make it through the coming ice age.

So it turns out you *can* toilet-train a bobcat.

The kind stranger who found Rufus in a parking lot thought he was a stray kitten. After an ill-fated attempt at bottle-feeding, the meaning of the cub's odd markings and large paws became clear, and the stranger, hands in bandages, brought the centre a new tenant.

Big cats are a lot like little cats, and the staff put the young bobcat in a large cage with a domestic tabby and her kittens. Arjun watched them compulsively, but the cub never seemed inclined to hurt his tiny foster siblings. Instead, he picked up some personal grooming tips and started using the sand-filled box in the corner.

Rufus loved to wrestle but let the smaller kitties win, rubbed his cheeks against the sides of the cage, and went wild over bits of pumpkin served mashed with his kibble. Early on, he tried to nurse and was rebuffed, but there was never any doubt that he was family. Looking at them together, I wondered if I'd missed some key developmental stage, the human equivalent of litter box 101. The tabby and her kittens were adopted out, and Rufus was transferred to a zoo in Minnesota when he outgrew our facility. Arjun wanted to visit him, and I said I'd go too.

"You planning to spring him out of jail?"

"Ha, nope. But we could swing by the Mall of America. I hear they've got a pirate ship."

Tell me a happy story.

Bear, salmon.

Tell me a sad story.

Salmon, bear.

What makes a story happy or sad? It depends on what happens to whom.

I envy Arjun for the way he is in the world, sharp, but without the jagged edges. He takes up exactly as much space as he needs to, while I waver between trying to disappear or insisting, too loudly, that I am here.

Jules, Arjun.

Arjun, Jules.

Road trip is two words. *Jailbreak* is one.

"Jules, do you want anything from India?"

"India?"

Arjun and I are hosing down the former raccoon enclosure. This was a good week—two releases, warm nights, no owls hit by trucks.

"Yeah, my uncle has an animation studio in Mumbai, and he wants me to work for him. I'm heading back next month to check it out, see how I feel about being home."

I know the expected responses for situations like this, the questions and the exclamations. But it takes me a little too long to get anything out. I find myself walking to the tap and giving it a hard twist, like it's stuck.

"I thought you liked it here," is what I manage.

Arjun grimaces at the smell of water meeting raccoon poop.

"I do, but I dunno. Sometimes it's nice to not have to worry about the other stuff. Visas. Work. The whole starving-artist BS. Hey . . . hey! Scoop *first*, then spray."

He sidesteps the dancing rubber coils and turns the spigot the other way.

"You not gonna miss Mamma Mia's?"

We each take a spade and start shovelling the little brown squiggles into a trash bag.

"Jules, we have pizza in India. We have Chinese food too. It's a big country."

"What about Rufus? What about Joan Wayne's farewell?"

I turn the hose full blast on a dark patch near the wall. Arjun hesitates between dodging the splash and moving in with a long-handled brush.

"Ahhhhh, they didn't tell you?" He opts for the brush. "Joan's being moved to a raptor centre up north. They train hawks to scare nuisance birds off runways."

I'm glad for the masks we're wearing in case of round-worms, though they make it hard to breathe. Arjun scrubs the floor like he means it.

"Come on, it's a good gig."

"What? Chasing seagulls or drawing cartoons?"

"Jules," he says, not taking the bait, "this isn't easy for me either. Home is . . . a bunch of things. You know."

Maybe it's the water droplets on his glasses and in his beard, but I'm thinking about the night after the reading and that fledgling tattoo wrapped like an arm around his torso, the beginnings of a story scratched into the skin. Back then I'd thought I would see this one through.

Arjun gathers the cleaning gear and picks up the trash bag as he steps out.

"Anyway, based on how our last two conversations went, I'll probably get in a fight with my dad and be back in three days."

"Wow. Oh wow," I say, turning around to lock up. "These raccoons aren't the only ones who are full of shit."

I'm not the only one who likes the lake in winter. Out on the ice, old men huddle in small groups or sit alone with a fishing line and a thermos. I hide behind the reeds near the shore, watching the children skate, fall, and slide on their bellies. A group of penguins in the water is called a raft. A group on land is called a waddle. Is lake ice land or water? If I were a child, I would be the one headed alone for the treeline on the far shore.

Cellphone batteries run down quickly in the cold. There's no reception so far from the city. If Arjun knocks on your door when you aren't home to hear it, does it still make a sound?

The last snow globe repairman in the world doesn't actually fix the broken figurines. Sometimes a dab of glue or paint suffices, but his storeroom, his whole home, is a warehouse of factory spares and replacements for when the damage is more extensive. I haven't talked to another human in two weeks.

Is this something that can be touched up with a brush? Or is there, in some waiting basement, a factory version of myself, colours vivid and still intact?

When I get home, I find a box of Japanese seaweed snacks outside my door. On it, a Post-it note says in Arjun's rounded hand: *KELP me! I'm drifting . . .*

The message comes with a sketch of a distressed sea otter, paws against its cheeks. I stick the yellow square on my fridge.

I've grown familiar with the sight of Joan Wayne's feet, pebbled and scaled like her dinosaur ancestors. Following these digits to their pointed conclusions, I imagine a rabbit or a vole, perhaps another of the centre's recent guests. Who are we saving, and for what?

I picture my own skin too, a tender perch sheathed in neither fur nor hide. She would draw blood without a thought. I try to visualize those claws gripping a thick leather glove, the kind worn by falconers. A cord connects her ankle to my wrist. But the mind rejects the image, turning instead to cliché: if you love someone, set them free.

After our shift, I tell Arjun I want to spend some extra time with Joan Wayne and will catch a ride with one of the staff. When his car is out of sight, I skirt the compound and head for the shed where they keep the sawdust and firewood. There's no reason for anyone to be here this late in the day, and they won't find me before locking up.

The centre has its evening rhythms, the thunk of plastic basins as people wash up, the clang of cage doors opening and closing. I sit on a pile of wood and wait for the sound of departing engines to fade. The air is several degrees colder now, and eventually I hear only forest noises. I don't want to risk turning on the lights, but even in the dark I know I can find the keys. There is some cage-rattling—inmates hopeful for a surprise night snack—but I'm in and out of the building quickly and standing before a familiar wire fence.

I've never been inside her enclosure, not even to clean it. To turn the key and push my way in feels like trespass.

Joan Wayne turns her head. The door is open, but I'm not sure if she sees that—the anticipation in the air is all mine. Her form is cloaked in the blue hues of evening, her eyes dark inside her silhouette. Do red-tailed hawks understand the concept of pointing? I've read that dogs do, but cats do not, and I'm not convinced that Joan is smarter than a cat. I gesture at the open door and beyond. She turns her head.

Her beak. They decided against releasing Joan because she'd grown too used to humans. Neither of us is safe with the other.

Time passes. Time stands still.

A breeze moves across my face, and she is gone. I fancy that I make out a dark shape climbing, but all I know for sure is that I'm the only one left. Something white and small and soft drifts out of the sky, but snow wasn't on the forecast. Bird fluff, then, tumbling off my face and down my jacket to be lost again.

"Jules, they know it was you."

I open the door for Arjun, then retreat inside. Morning is in the windows, and the snow globes look milky in the light. I go back to wiping down their outsides, sending up little swirls and eddies.

"They couldn't reach you, so they called me. And your phone was off, so . . ."

I thought I saw a scratch on Dorothy's globe, but it buffed out with some attention.

"Jules, she came back. Joan Wayne came back. They saw the door, and people were yelling, and we checked the woods and . . . They set out some food in her usual spot and she came back. It sometimes takes a few days, but they come back, Jules."

Dorothy in her blue dress infuriates me. A new world and a wish to be granted. Of all things to choose.

Why do you want to go back? I ask the porcelain figure. What about your new life?

I should have bought a Magic 8-Ball instead, at least there'd be hope of a different outcome.

Be brave, Dorothy, be brave. Why can't you be brave?

I shake her, I reason with her, I send her flying across the room.

In one version of the story, the globe hits the floor with a crack like the end of the world. I half expect there to be water and glass everywhere, but the ball just rolls over and trickles weakly, like a small wounded animal.

Arjun knows it was never meant to hit him. But he's said what he had to, and he's gone.

The last snow globe repairman in the world is in Northfield, Minnesota, a three-hour drive from the town where I live. In this version of the story, I make the journey in a blizzard, two hundred miles to knock on an old man's door. He is surprised, but kind, and lets me in.

"What can I do for you?" he asks in a voice that sounds like *musique*.

The entire way, the globe was leaking into my clothes as it sat on my lap. I clutch it to my chest as the dark stain spreads, and I say to him: "Please, fix this. Fix this."

In one version of the story, we are eating pizza on the couch. Arjun's boots are leaving puddles on my wooden floor. Inside the Taj Mahal snow globe on the window ledge, a banner proclaims "Indian Summer" in gold and glitter. Outside, a couple struggles with what looks like a month's worth of groceries and eight gallons of bottled water.

It's all over the radio: Snowmageddon, Snowpocalypse, the coming of a new ice age.

Getting up, Arjun and I touch our noses to the pane, palms against the glass.

The first time I saw snow, I had just moved to the Midwest. I was eighteen and still going to parties—we were in a freshman dorm, all of us had eaten a cautious but sufficient number of the pills the boy with the green eyeshadow had been giving out, and were off in our separate but connected realities. One of the boys was convinced he was a cat.

"I'm a cat! Meow, meow, meow!"

"Meow!" I replied. "Meow, meow!"

We held this conversation for an indeterminate amount of time. Then he said, "I'm a doll!" He froze for a moment into an attitude of stiffness, then crumpled onto the floor. I could no longer talk to him, so I fell asleep.

We didn't all get up at once, but when we did, we didn't speak, didn't go anywhere, so eventually we were all sitting up and staring outside the window, and it was snowing. Then someone said, "It's snowing!" And so the spell broke, or rather, one spell ended and another began. How shall I put it—the world had turned on its side as we were sleeping, and the air was full of tiny fugitives, trying to find their place.

CARA MARKS

AURORA BOREALIS

1. You pour me another drink
I love the sound of liquid falling—a river splashing on stone, that pitter-patter of rain on the skylight, the mellifluous comfort of more wine in my cup. To let go of something impossible to hold on your own, with bare hands. To fill yourself up.

We sit on a wooden swing in the garden with swirly blue and yellow mugs that remind me of Greece, though I've never been. They're filled with Okanagan Pink Pinot Gris and freshly picked mint and raspberries. You're tipsy and want me to join you. You're sad. You're a mature man of new masculinity, think you're tougher if you show your feelings. But still you don't want to cry in front of me, your youngest child and only daughter. The boys have already gone home.

"The garden is beautiful," I say, because it is. It is barely edible—filled with Mama's flowers: clematis, chrysanthemums, zinnias, dahlias, a million ferns. Plum, pear, apple trees with fruit not yet ripe. A corkscrew willow by a dory-sized pond. No lawn or lawnmower.

You wear a bathrobe without shirt or trousers. Socked feet slipped into flip-flops, legs crossed, your hair a thinning white side-parted mop. You wear Mama's glasses because yours are broken. The lenses are smudged. In your lap, you hold a pink carnation and your cup. Are we going to get drunk? There are two jugs full of wine and a bucket of berries. You sip and sip, roll a raspberry on your tongue.

The swing sits three and lazily sways, and I wonder how to approach the space between us. You are too far away to lean into, and I don't know how to give you comfort, if that is what you need. The sunlight staggers out of blushing clouds. The pond's edges stitched with apple blossoms, its musty smell intertwined with the flowers' sweetness.

I check my watch and say, "Soon we'll have cake."

Odd, to be surrounded by lush foliage not yet decaying, all these things we didn't plant.

2. *Mama sings a Spanish ballad*

A month ago, a week before she died, Mama stood in the garage with a paintbrush and an enormous canvas where a car could be. She was sixty-three and I was about to be thirty. Her hair all grey curls tucked under a teal scarf, tied above her forehead. She wore a denim smock over bare legs, naked feet splattered with paint. I sat on the floor, tiptoeing onto the canvas when I stretched out my legs. She painted Frida Kahlo flowers and snow-capped mountains and the northern lights. Her song delicate, her voice a coloratura contralto, and I didn't understand the words, only *bella bella bella*, which she sang over and over and twirled, pink paint from her brush Pollocking the canvas and the walls.

"Do you like it?" she said, and stood in a dizzy sway. "It's not done yet."

She dropped into child's pose and leaned into the canvas, her knees and forearms freshly painted. She had always painted but wanted to be a poet. In cursive at the bottom corner of the canvas she wrote in baby blue with a skinny brush:

> *my bella— sweetness*
> *you are an O'Keeffe landscape,*
> *Rothko in the summer,*
> *Matisse in the morning*
> *you are the great and wild*
> *unknown known and*
> *I love you*

But how to say it, she would say, how to write love into poetry without using the word. *Love*, the word, weighs down a poem, she'd been told. How to tell me she loved me. And yet I always knew.

"You can have it for your birthday," she said.

"Where will I put it?"

She stretched out her arms, a crucifix covered in pink.

"Has he called?" I asked.

She crooked her head, tugged off the teal. She rose again with her feet at her insignia. "You can use it as a rug."

3. I pour you another as well and you yodel and we remember
We are drunk now. You are doing that thing with your hands where you twist the tip of each finger as if a cork you wish to

unscrew, where really you just want a cigarette but you haven't smoked since 1983.

The sky bleeds off its colour and the swing rocks swifter now. You have removed your glasses and I wonder, Can you still see me?

You guzzle the new wine in your mug and totter to the pond's edge.

I leave you there, for a moment, and meander to the kitchen to find the cake. I'm distracted by flowers along the way. I pick an enormous pale pink dahlia. The flower's twirled petals are soft and it's the size of my face. You've left your suitcase on the dining-room table and a pile of your clothes on the floor. I ease open the oven and am engulfed in its warmth and the smell of ginger and cinnamon. The cake has burnt because we are drunk and when I return to the garden you have jumped into the pond. You're up to your waist in milky green water and you splash and splash.

"*Yodelayheehoo,*" you sing. "*Yodelayheehooooooo.*"

I tell you to get out, you'll drown, but I know you will not drown because the water is at your waist and I say you'll get hypothermia but it is September and it is a hot September and you are warm with wine and death is not your concern, not yours.

You say, "You have never loved."

"The cake is burnt," I say, and again you say *You have never loved*.

"*Yodelayheeeehoooohoohoooooo-ooo-ooo-oo.*"

The cake is burnt but I hold it, I carry it on Grandma's bright orange plate with a bowl of whisky-spiced whipped cream, to cover the burn. It's Mama's recipe, and your favourite at

Christmas, and the only thing I can bake and yet I can't, couldn't quite. It is ginger cake and there was not enough ginger. I cracked one too many eggs and I did not wait for the butter to rest at room temperature. And yet I baked it.

I stand, unsteady, amid zinnias. Their gold and red blossoms at my knees. I place the cake and the cream in the middle of the swing with two forks.

"The cake is burnt but there is cake," I say, "and I loved her."

"But why loved," you say. "Why *love-duh*."

"Dad, you're going to catch a cold."

"It was so easy for you."

"Please would you get out of there? You are so wet."

"It's raining," you say, and it has just begun to.

4.Can you hear the northern lights?

In August, Mama visited me in Squamish and we drove her pickup truck to Whitehorse to see you, to see if you would come home. We drove for two days straight because she could not wait.

She wanted to see the sun, how many hours it would stay in the sky, and when it fell she hoped for the aurora borealis. She said it was bioluminescence in the sky, but I'd always thought bioluminescence looked like stars. She told me this at 3 a.m., parked on the side of the road an hour past Kitwanga, when we were both too tired to drive. I staggered almost into a dream and when I woke the engine rumbled and it was barely 5 a.m., Mama in her fuchsia coat with her hood on, humming quietly.

We arrived at Uncle F.'s and found you on the front porch. The cabin surrounded by pines, its foundation tipping toward the slow river. You played guitar, barefoot in a black suit and a bomber hat.

Mama tripped out of the truck to kiss you, but you said, "What are you doing here?"

Mama said she loved you and you asked again, *Why are you here.*

Uncle F. swung open the screen door and gave Mama and me kisses on the cheek. He smacked your head like he'd have done when you were kids and told you to get up.

You went there to hunt, to stay with Uncle F. and eat fresh moose, fresh fish. You killed a bison and packed its meat—we no longer called it a body—in brown paper in the freezer. Mama said, "What will you do with all this meat?" She'd been a vegetarian for forty years.

That night we listened to Bruce Springsteen and you and Uncle F. shotgunned cheap beer. Mama and I drank honeyed tea. Uncle F. smoked a cigarillo and called himself sophisticated. Mama held Jackal, the grey tabby cat, in her lap. We sat there, on the porch, waiting to see the light show—emerald, mauve, red ribbons shimmering by the stars. We wondered if it would come, if it would be enough. Mama fell asleep and you carried her to the sofa in the early morning. Uncle F. fell asleep too, but we left him there. We lay with our backs on the oak floor of the porch, Jackal on your belly, rising and falling with your breath.

You said, "I'm not ready," and I let it linger.

I tried to find constellations, decipher abstract patterns and find their ancient myths and truths. Orion, Ursa Major, but that's all I found. Hazy green shone in the sky like headlights in fog and I asked was this it, should I wake up Mama?

You said these were barely them, it wasn't worth it to wake her up.

I fell asleep there too and woke to you and Mama whispering in the kitchen, Mama's hushed tears, a caw of a crow, and the quiet rush of the river. You held each other, her face tucked into the lapels of your suit.

On the way home we stopped in Stewart again and Mama asked me to wait for a minute. She wanted to hike to the glacier, to touch it. It looked so close but took her hours to get there and back. The glacier stretched out between mountains and looked like the sky. I sat in the truck and waited. She shrunk, became a little pink bird flying away and away to touch the clouds.

"I'm sorry," she said, and I said it was fine, we have days to get home, and she said sorry for being hard to love. She said, "I think your dad finds me too hard to love."

I wondered what you'd say, why you stayed in Whitehorse, and what you both meant by love.

FAWN PARKER

FEED MACHINE

I was impatient because my therapist, whose name was Melba, asked me to arrive at her home office at 11:45 and when I arrived at 11:44, she was around back throwing seed at two ducks floating in her above-ground pool. The ducks floated still like buoys and did not react to the seed. Melba shouted, "You know you want it," and threw another handful at the ducks. The seed was tossed back at her by the wind.

I normally saw Melba on Thursdays, but this was a Saturday. She'd asked me to join her and another patient with a similar problem to mine on an excursion in lieu of my usual weekly appointment. The excursion was a trip to the science centre, where we would view an exhibit called The Living Body.

The other patient's name was Nevaeh, like Heaven backward, and she was nine. Nevaeh was a patient of Melba's, but she was also Melba's granddaughter. Nevaeh's mother had terminal brain cancer and was scheduled to die.

On the way to The Living Body exhibit Nevaeh and I sat in the back of Melba's Jeep and didn't look at each other. Melba let us take turns choosing songs on her MP3 player, which she transmitted through an FM adapter in her cigarette lighter receptacle. I chose "Season of the Witch" by Donovan and Nevaeh chose "Hurdy Gurdy Man," also by Donovan, because I guess she didn't know any of the artists in Melba's music library. The songs came through very weakly and with a lot of static.

"Good choice," I said to Nevaeh, and she said nothing.

Melba paid for Nevaeh's ticket to The Living Body exhibit and I paid for my own. Nevaeh followed us around the circuit of displays with her hands cupped around her eyes like blinders so she would not see anything she did not want to see. She communicated to Melba by whispering and mostly ignored me. Nevaeh had a small black agenda she carried with her. In the agenda Melba made Nevaeh write a small letter *B* each time she binged and a small letter *P* each time she purged. Before we entered the exhibition room, Nevaeh opened her agenda and drew a small circle or perhaps a letter *O* or perhaps a numeral zero under that current day's date. There was other, neater, writing in the agenda that said things like *Chicken breast, Hotdog,* and *Gatorade.* It was adult cursive, but not like Melba's, which I knew from my tax receipts. I wondered if Nevaeh's terminal mother kept track of Nevaeh's food diary for her, and how all of that would go moving forward, and I felt depressed. I wondered what Nevaeh talked about in her sessions with Melba.

Once in a session, Melba asked me if I was uncomfortable with my sexuality and I said yes. She asked me what sorts of things made me uncomfortable, and I said, "Certain phrases," and she said, "Like what?" and I hesitated and she said, "Go on," and I said, "When somebody says let me see that . . ." and she said, "Let me see that what? " and I said, "I don't want to say," and she said, "Let me see that . . . ?" and I said, "That . . ." and she said, "That . . . ?" and I said, "Pussy."

Melba said that sexual avoidance and preoccupation with weight are related for some people and that I was one of those people. She said that it was important to pay attention to what did and didn't make me uncomfortable. Then we watched *Goodbye to Love*, the movie about Karen Carpenter and how she died from being anorexic, and I thought about how my voice had cracked earlier when I'd said "pussy" and how that had made me uncomfortable. Melba asked me at the end of the session to say "Let me see that pussy" out loud, and I did it. "Let me see that pussy," I said to Melba, and she said, "Good."

I liked having Nevaeh with us because it meant that Melba wouldn't talk to me about Karen Carpenter or about men. Instead she asked Nevaeh yes-or-no questions about school and Nevaeh nodded or shook her head. Melba asked Nevaeh if she had any plans to see her friends that weekend, and Nevaeh shook her head no.

"I like your macramé bracelet," I said to Nevaeh because I wanted to make her feel not ugly. She smiled ferociously, and then slapped her hands over her mouth.

Melba said, "Look," and pointed to a glass case. Inside was an artificial cross-section of a human body. The display was labelled "Feed Machine." Melba said, "Feed Machine."

Nevaeh looked deeply sad approaching the Feed Machine. She returned her hands to the sides of her face and then turned her head to the side so as not to see the Feed Machine.

"Hold Nevaeh's hand while I'm in the bathroom," said Melba.

I reached for Nevaeh's hand and she put it inside of mine, which was much larger than hers. She had dry skin with red sores on her knuckles and around her fingernails. Her cuticles were torn and bloody and her nails were bitten down to the quick. I held her hand very gently and it felt at risk of slipping right out. It also felt like holding on to a crumpled paper bag.

"Nevaeh," I said, and Nevaeh turned her head away from me but wrapped her fingers around my hand to suggest she was listening. "I hate the Feed Machine."

Nevaeh, I could tell, did another one of her ferocious smiles.

"The Feed Machine is our enemy," I said.

Neveah turned her head back to me and tilted it up in the way she tilted it at Melba when she wanted to whisper to her. I leaned down so Nevaeh could whisper to me, and she very quietly whispered, "Yes."

"I want the Feed Machine to feel the immense pain that we feel," I said to Nevaeh. "Plus some."

Melba returned from the bathroom. "Do you want to feed the Feed Machine?' she said. She rubbed her hands together in excitement, like a villain.

"Yes," I said. "We do."

There was a spout on the left of the glass case around the machine, and beside the spout was a bowl of produce. Nevaeh was too small to reach the produce so I picked out a green apple and gave it to her, and picked out a green bell pepper for myself, and Melba picked out a peach. Melba dropped her peach into the spout and a conveyor belt delivered the peach into the artificial body's cross-sectional mouth, and the peach was ground up by a series of gears and rotating barbed metal cylinders inside of the torso. The machine made a chopping noise when it processed the peach pit. Nevaeh covered her ears and turned away.

"Help Nevaeh feed the machine," said Melba.

"Okay," I said. I lifted Nevaeh so that she could drop her green apple into the spout, and then I put her down. I wanted to apologize for controlling her, but she had heard Melba tell me to do it, so I felt that she understood. Nevaeh's apple was processed by the machine and moved through the system shortly after the peach. The peach now was near the bottom of the intestines, and it was no longer recognizably a peach but more of a wet, brown mass. The wet, brown mass of peach matter arrived at the end of the intestine, the ass, and was dispensed into an oval hole in the floor beneath the artificial ass. It was then followed by Nevaeh's apple. I put my green bell pepper back into the bowl of produce.

"Look at that system," said Melba.

The way she said *that* system reminded me of how I'd said *that* pussy to her. This pussy, I thought to myself. Fuck this pussy. I imagined a similar machine to the Feed Machine, called the Fuck Machine, in another more private area of The Living Body exhibit. "Do you want to fuck the Fuck Machine?' Melba would say. "Yes," I would say. "I want *that cock* to fuck *this pussy*."

Another small girl who probably was Nevaeh's age pressed her face against the glass case on the opposite side from us, and her nose got scrunched up like a pig's. The other girl was fairly overweight, which was fine, but I did notice. Nevaeh also pressed her face against the glass, and scrunched her nose into a pig's nose, and put her dry bloody hands flat on the glass also, and the girls stared at one another, and I looked away so that they could live their lives.

Melba was reading a guide she'd taken from the lobby. She showed it to me and pointed at the middle page and read, "*The Body in Society.* 12:30."

"I think," I said, "that I will go with Nevaeh to the food court while you watch *The Body in Society.* If that is okay?'

"Yes," Melba said, "great idea."

When Nevaeh heard me say her name, she backed away from the glass and turned to me. The other girl was gone. I walked Nevaeh out of the main exhibition room directly through the crowd of other visitors so that she would not need her blinders and would not see anything she did not want to see.

In the food court I ordered four square-shaped slices of pepperoni pizza and two Cokes and one slice of Oreo cheese-cake to go, and held the to-go container in one hand and held on to Nevaeh's scaly hand with the other.

"I want to kill the Feed Machine," I said to Nevaeh. She looked up at my face and then at the to-go container. Then Nevaeh pulled her hand out of my hand. I worried I had upset her by saying the word *kill.*

"I am sorry for being hostile," I said. "The Feed Machine makes me feel worked up."

Nevaeh shook her arm violently, the one attached to the hand I had been holding. Her macramé bracelet fell off onto the floor and she bent and picked it up and held it out to me.

"Thank you," I said, and I put her macramé bracelet on my wrist and it fit. I felt immense relief that the bracelet was not too small for me. If the bracelet had not fit I would have felt that I had let Nevaeh down, by being overweight like the young girl on the other side of the glass case.

Nevaeh tilted her head as if to whisper again, and I leaned forward and she said nothing. She had changed her mind.

"I am going to make the machine have a letter *B*," I said. "And then we will write it in the machine's agenda."

Nevaeh scratched at the back of her hand and it started to bleed. She put the skin up to her mouth and sucked on it. I looked away so that she would feel like I had not noticed.

The other girl returned to the Feed Machine. She came to stand at Nevaeh's side and Nevaeh continued to suck on her hand skin. I felt respectfully invisible to the two of them.

I opened the to-go container and stacked the four square-shaped slices of pizza on top of one another like book pages, like an agenda full of letter *B*s. I put all four into the Feed Machine's spout, and then I opened the Coke cans and poured Coke into the spout, and then I fed the machine the slice of Oreo cheesecake.

Melba approached the glass case. "*The Body in Society*," she said. "Fascinating. The body can be an instrument of freedom, or it can be a prison."

"Like a glass case," I said. "The Feed Machine is in double prison. For being bad."

Melba looked into the glass case at the Feed Machine. "Yum," she said. "It's the machine's lucky day."

I thought about Melba feeding the Feed Machine seed, like the ducks in her pool.

Nevaeh pulled at the macramé bracelet around my wrist. I took it off and returned it to her, and she offered it to the other girl. The other girl held out her hand so Nevaeh could put the bracelet on her, but the bracelet was too small for the other girl's wrist.

Nevaeh's hands worked like gory spiders unravelling the macramé and then tying a series of chunky knots around the other girl's wrist. It was tight like the string tied around a pot roast. I wondered if Nevaeh tied it so tight to punish the girl, but the girl looked at the macramé bracelet on her wrist and grinned, and Nevaeh grinned and whispered something to the girl.

Melba and the girls and I stood around the exhibit's case with our faces pressed up against the glass. The mass worked its way through the intestines and the machine made a sound like an audience cheering underwater. Drowning. The binge food reached the end of the system and the Feed Machine took a large but normal shit into the hole at the bottom of the display. I wanted to laugh, but no one else did, so I stayed still like the ducks being rained on by seed.

JOHN ELIZABETH STINTZI

COVEN COVETS BOY

On the back of Volume 48 of her series of diaries Sandy wrote: *"your that dreamy."—David W.* in large sans serifs with a red permanent marker, as if it were a blurb from the *New York Times*. The excerpted quote came from a text message David W. had sent her, in which those words were a shunt from the context. David W.'s full quote ran:

Oh come on Sandy. Not even your that dreamy.

Sandy, in her seventeenth year, took David W.'s words not with a grain of salt but through a sieve. She let all the possible iterations of David W.'s digitized inflection squeeze away, allowed each word to stand dry in the glory of its own merits, bearing with it textbook definitions.

Dreamy: |ˈdriːmi| *adjective.*
1. Having a magical or dreamlike quality.
—This song that is playing on the radio is quite dreamy.
2. A word you use to describe the person you're in love with.
—Sandy [. . .] your that dreamy.

David W. was the second hottest boy at Sandy's school. The hottest was Brice Q., who had all the natural, anthropological qualities of attraction. He was taller, he had superior muscle tone, his hair was wavier and smooth and always clean. Brice Q. was popular and smart.

Brice Q.'s backswing in tennis was almost as legendary as his backside in tennis shorts. In almost every girls' bathroom in town there were printouts of iPhone pics, photocopies of Polaroids shot on expired cartridges, newspaper clippings of Brice Q. stuck to the walls of select stalls with chewing gum and double-sided tape. There was even, on top of a ceiling tile in Stall #3 of the girls' bathroom near Mr. Bartlett's class, a white towel stained in Brice Q.'s sweat, which he discarded after an intense final set against a high school down in Waterloo. Three vans of his fans had followed him there, though only one was able to take the towel back. The girls in the chosen van remembered that trip as a pilgrimage, while the others remembered it as a mistake of destiny. A test of faith.

Every now and again, in the bathroom, a tall girl would climb atop the toilet's cistern and carry the towel down from the ceiling, pass it around to the others like a priest passing out the Eucharist. While the old faucets dripped through the quiet, the girls took turns burrowing their faces into the dusty, pheromone-crusted folds.

The only girls' bathroom frequented by teenagers in which there was not any sort of shrine to Brice Q. was the bathroom at the local bowling alley, The Lois Lanes, where almost every lane was warping, splotched with wax-less patches. There, on dead Sunday afternoons, Sandy and her coven would gather to discuss the second hottest boy, David W.—the inferno in their fledgling hearts.

Their rituals of devotion did not include photographs, did not involve overwhelming their senses with idols or iconography. They did not have a collection of relics to pass around, but instead they shared memories, moments. Some, like Sandy, brought in their diaries to read from, some brought printouts of blog posts they'd written and published online— where they changed all the names and pretended they lived in strange places like Paris and Boise. Two simply came in and followed the oral tradition, would just stare at the ceiling and shed the words as they came. There were only six of them in all—five girls, one boy.

On Sundays, in the bathroom of The Lois Lanes, they'd each recite stories featuring David W.–like psalms. One of the six would go into a stall, stand or sit on the toilet, door open or shut, and read or recite while the others stood scattered around the rest of the bathroom, eyes often closed, leaning back against sink taps and stall walls, heads bobbing, possessed hands navigating their solitary topographies, each word an incantation. Stories of being brushed by in the halls. Stories of steam-stained dreams. Stories—from the boy—of David W. in the gym locker room nudely whipping other boys with his wet towel, of the boy's harrowing attempts to hide his desire. They were beating-heart stories, stories like witnessing fight after fight between David W. and Principal Wayne over grades and pranks and tardiness. Stories of David W. looking at one of the coven girls and smirking, and even once sticking his tongue out at her when he caught her staring at him for the third time during a study hour before lunch, and then finally—after class—walking over and saying hello, his maroon uniform untucked from his shorts. The small beginnings of a blond moustache, which was visible only from a foot away or closer, punching out from his semi-coarse skin.

This girl, of course: Sandy.

With keen attention, it was possible to see the palpable magnetism of Brice Q. when he came down the hallways or bent down to pick up a book from the bottom of his locker. Bodies angled toward him as they passed, eyes ever glancing and grazing and surveying on the sly. When he was not at his locker, girls would reach out and touch the door as they passed.

After school, when he was training for a match in the gym, or on the court outside—or when he was studying for a final in the library—folded love notes would be stuffed into his locker through the little grate at the top. Every morning, when he opened his locker, the notes would tumble out like perfumed leaves in fall. He only ever smiled at them and put them in his pockets. He had never been known to read them. His head had always seemed to live elsewhere.

David W.'s locker was on the other side of school. The top hinge was broken so that it barely shut, releasing an aroma of dull smoke and mildew. Those who watched him did so from a distance. Unlike Brice Q.'s, David W.'s eyes were always on the lookout, trying to catch the glances that came his way. He stared out sharp from his spindle of bangs.

When he'd caught Sandy, when he had fully encircled her, she thought he would never let her go.

Volumes 26 through 58 of Sandy's diary series, an accelerated pace ranging from Sandy at sixteen to eighteen, show the spectrum of Sandy's obsession with David W.

Throughout, his role fluctuates. He begins as a casual mention, transitions into a minor character (whose use is largely to contrast others, like Brice Q. or herself), then quickly—in Volume 28—becomes a catalyst for Sandy's metamorphosis into a girl mature enough to fall in love with the second hottest boy. Volume 30 talks about the coven, outlines its meetings, takes notes of all the stories shared there.

From that point, David W. begins to turn, starts displacing Sandy as main character, relegating her into something little other than the speaker or—farther off—his author. In Volumes 33 through 46—written in a few frantic months—there is almost no mention of Sandy's life at all, except insofar as its function as a witness to him. The diaries begin to read like a field book, as if an imperceptible Jane Goodall had been airdropped into Sandy's school and had followed the somewhat chimpish David W. from room to room, watching him smoke and spit, pinning down his existence page by page, learning his habits of feeding, fighting, and love.

In Volume 47—after the Hello—Sandy steps out from the

authorial sphere as a possible love interest, and David W. begins to contort into a possible anti-hero. Volume 48 is giddy and befuddled and blurbed. Volume 50 plays with the idea of David W. as a somewhat malevolent god, and Sandy as benevolent minion or casual girlfriend. Volume 51 is completely devoted to a long night in the fall of Sandy's seventeenth year. Volume 53, the first written almost entirely in red ink, toys around with the idea of David W. as a comic book super villain. Of Sandy as the represesntative dead on page 4.

The last five volumes—54 through 58—the rubble of old screams.

After David W. first kissed Sandy, the coven was still with her. It was widely construed by each of the other members as an accident of darkness and proximity during the 1st of July celebrations of Sandy's seventeenth year. There'd been a large group of girls and boys at the edge of the trees in the park that night, including the rest of the coven. Every other body was a chance for an excuse. They each believed it could have happened to any of them.

Sandy described the kiss, late in Volume 49, as a magic, aching moment. For the sake of the coven, she shared details about the feel of the fuzz of his face, the bony clasp of his fist on her shoulder, his smoke-sewn tongue twigging into her mouth like a blinded snake. She described him as his physical manifestation rather than an ethereal blast. For herself, in Volume 49, she wrote the effects on the beat of her melodramatic heart:

It was as if an instant had taken me into its arms, as if the
lips of his lips and the lips of mine had spoken while our real
true heart-lips were unable to part.

———— ◦◦◦◦ ————

After the kiss, the orbit that the coven had kept around
David W. began to tighten. His magnetism increased with the
knowledge of his capabilities. The coven started to inch closer
to him, to try and fall into the same net of his eyes that Sandy
had been trapped in.

At their meetings, they listened to Sandy talk about how
he had driven her home from school one rainy day in his dad's
old Ford, how he had confessed to her that he had been the
one to slice the tires of Brice Q.'s Honda, how he had given
her a cigarette that made her sick, and they began taking
notes. They listened to her and drew close to her. On a week-
night, two weeks into Sandy's senior year, the boy went to
her house to study chemistry with her and when she went to
the bathroom he wrote down all the names of the perfume
bottles on her dresser, recorded her bra size, the material
of her clothes—anything of hers that could have been part of
David W.'s apparent attraction—and reported everything
back to the others.

Slowly, without Sandy realizing, they started to dress very
similar to her. They matched her gait, wore bras too small or
too large, began smoking in secret. The boy began bathing in
water infused with the perfume to get a hint of her scent.
They each were trying to turn David W.'s head away from
Sandy and toward them. They wanted to be interchangeable.

One heart subbed in for another. They wanted to believe themselves capable of being beloved too.

After Sandy made love to David W., during the September of her senior year, three months before her birthday—Volume 51—the coven was no longer with her. She stood on the toilet in The Lois Lanes bathroom, reading the scene from the diary: the fear, the shifter, the moon eclipsing between blinks—the bareness of cock—the short trickle of blood and his clucking after, punctuating and gibbous. The calm quiet drive home. The second hand job in her parents' driveway before she stepped out of the truck.

When Sandy came out of the trance of her story and left the altar of the stall, the bathroom was empty. The taps were turned full on.

The coven was not with Sandy again until they'd each been made love to, and thoroughly fucked. Over the course of her senior year, each husk slowly became reverent of her, the prophet, the first victim of his tricks, each one except the boy, who moved with his worried mother to Manitoba after David W. and three of his goons pummelled him in the schoolyard after homecoming, after he'd been caught smiling at David W. several times from the dance floor. But by then, everything was already too late. There was too much blood and pain in being tethered together by hate, there was too much pain in being tethered together at all.

Without the coven, they did not speak of what happened to them. They all knew intimately the price they had paid in falling victim to the cult of personality, of wanting to please the perceived unpleaseable, to charm the vulnerable, misunderstood kid they believed hid beyond the wall. Split from the coven due to envy, they did not have the resources to learn from each other, to know the signs, to know not to accept the six packs, the invitations to take a long drive to hang out by the water.

They did not have the chance to shake the clouds from each other's eyes, to try and devise ways to stop the hungry encroachment of a hand on the thigh. They did not learn the cost of surrendering to a smoky man behind a mask, did not have the chance to be warned that David W. was not misunderstood at all. That he had been there, on the surface, the whole time.

Divided, they could each be conquered with routine tactics.

⁂

During the Snowball dance of Sandy's senior year, long after the coven had burst into individuals, the cathedrals to Brice Q.—at the other end of the school from the gymnasium, where the dance was held—were raided. Photos, originals and copies printed out and stashed there, were torn to shreds and flushed into flooding clods that the school's plumbing couldn't pass. Red paint was splashed on the scrawled-on stall walls with a wide brush, walls where hundreds of one-sided hearts— B.Q. & __. __.—were drawn in. Splashes and spills from the red paint mixed with the overflowing water and drained under the doors into the halls. Principal Wayne and the janitors, when it was discovered the next morning, panicked, fearing death. The sweat-filled towel was also plucked from its reliquary atop the ceiling tile, never to return.

It was the beginning of a silent upheaval, broken out from the tail end of betrayal. After that dance Brice Q.'s idolaters were thrown into a fog from the violent erasing. To them, Brice Q. became a bit less visible, began to be seen as he was in the singular present and not as he was stacked upon and tacked beside himself.

The deprogramming of the myth of Brice Q. started from this systematic removal of the icons from bathrooms around town. A few zealots were able to preserve their ideas of Brice Q., but mostly they were shook from him. Suddenly, without photos, he breathed, grew angles and depths that were imperceptible in the inked flatness. Suddenly, without access to his pheromones, people began to grow an immunity to him. They listened to him speak and got bored when he didn't sound like Lancelot.

Destabilized and dragged back into the present, they began to dismantle their own, private cathedrals. They followed suit the invisible, unnameable hands.

⁂

Sandy's diaries ended at Volume 58, around two-thirds of the way in. The day was February 14 of Sandy's eighteenth year. She wrote it in third person, wrote about Sandy's loneliness, the destructive anxiety that had descended on her, its acuteness since she learned that David W. had been expelled by

Principal Wayne, how he was free to wander the world unscheduled. She wrote about how far Sandy felt from being understood, how over the weekend she had read through all the old diaries she'd written and realized that she didn't understand Sandy either.

Her parents were out for the night, having a romantic dinner, and Sandy sat in front of the lit fireplace in the living room. The fire was roiling from the tail end of the fuel of Volume 57, and the whole room seemed to flutter, paper ash scooting through the air like dry grey snow. There, sweating, heart racing, she wrote about Sandy through to the end of her diaried-life, ending Volume 58 like a journalist who ran out of letters mid-word.

I don't think Sandy was ever made to love or be loved. This is not how a life is supposed to work, cracked off two mo

Then, she let the flames finish it.

⠶⠶⠶

Years later an email chain opened up to the six of them, arriving from the far edge of a long silence, to addresses they'd hardly used or checked since graduating from high school and moving on, to university in Toronto (for philosophy) and New Brunswick (for nursing) and Brandon (for education), or to working in resorts at the lake, or—for one girl, the fourth of them—to raising a child alone, still living in her parents' home. The email came from David W.'s second, the girl who'd written the blog set in Boise, which she deleted two weeks after he'd quit returning her calls. The email started with an apology and ended with an invitation to reconnect. She talked

JOHN ELIZABETH STINTZI   121

about how she had just got out of a stint in the hospital because of an eating disorder following a bad, bad relationship. She said she still thought about them all the time. She asked them what they were doing, what their addresses were, and whether they were doing okay.

Three girls and one boy responded, replying all, in longer and shorter form.

A few weeks later, the final response came in the form of five small packages arriving to five different stoops across the country. There were no words in any of them, no return address, there was nothing but a single plastic baggie.

Within each baggie was one-sixth of an old, white towel.

SUSAN SANFORD BLADES

THE REST OF HIM

air work-slicked and tie sagging, Nik lifts my covers and pokes me with a corner of envelope. From your mom, he says. He thanks me, with a generous helping of sarcasm, for ensuring our daughter got off to school on time, then informs me he has floor hockey with the boys tonight and I should not wait up. What grown man plays floor hockey?

Of course, after being incommunicado for sixteen years, Mom sends me a newspaper article about Dad's severed foot. No note, no marginalia, not even penned devil's horns on his image. He's been dead to her for years, no need for fanfare.

I decide to leave the house with my mail and no plans to return. We'll see who shouldn't wait up for whom. My daughter's fifteen now—as long as she's got a buzzing rectangle of light in her palms, she doesn't care if I'm here or there. Nik's going through his Sad Man phase and is no help at all. Sears went under four years ago and he hasn't worked since. He's not fancy enough for The Bay, too proud for Walmart. The only thing he's ever done is manage the men's department. His only skill is loyalty, and I'm even less qualified. Now we live off EI and his mother's pity. We haven't told our daughter and Nik doesn't intend to. Every morning, he dresses for work and we slump off to hide out in separate coffee shops. I buy almond lattes in white mugs from a Scandinavian-looking couple with clear eyes and unclenched jaws. Nik buys Americanos in paper cups from young, dark-haired women with tattooed heads and effusive problems. I'll walk by his café of choice, saddled with legumes and leafy greens, and see him through the window, elbows to counter, body curled toward a shady pixie, nodding gracefully like he used to for me. It's easier to listen to troubles you can walk away from.

In Little Norway, the curly haired wife delivers my almond latte and a cup of sparkling water and toast and jam for Jenny across the table. The wife has freckled, doughy cheeks and is braless under a black-and-white striped European boat shirt. How could anyone stray from a woman with cheeks like that?

Jenny's all, Mmmph shoo good, with the jam. It's home-made, you know, she says.

I nod and pop bubbles in my water with my fingertip.

Jenny licks a bright red glob off her palm and tells me she thinks she's dating a married man.

You think he's married, or you think you're dating?

Both.

Does he wear a ring?

Jenny nods but gives me jazz hands. It could be decorative.

On his ring finger?

It's big and twisty. Not a band. Definitely.

Have you kissed?

Jenny taps her cheek and presses her tongue into it.

Beej?

She flicks crumbs at me. He kissed me on the cheek.

I wouldn't want Nik doing that.

Men will be assholes.

You want to date an asshole?

If you cut out the assholes, what's left?

Flaccid, too-nice guys.

Jenny gags into my water glass. Right, she says, khaki pants, duck-footed walk.

European man-bag.

Feathered hair.

Smiles at children in restaurants.

Those are the closet Paul Bernardos.

Are you seeing him tonight?

Jenny shrugs. He's kind of spur-of-the-moment.

Mind if I stay with you?

Jenny raises her eyebrows.

My dad died.

You have parents?

My mom mailed me this article.

I uncrumple the clipping. There's Dad onstage, hands groping a mic as though it was a cliff edge he was falling from.

Jenny's in her glazy-eyed new man world and doesn't notice the headline. All she says is, Your dad's cute.

I read the headline: "LOCAL PUNK PIONEER LEAVES PODIATRIC PUZZLE." Some hiker found my dad's foot on the beach.

Where's the rest of him?

"Feet disarticulate from the body as a result of prolonged immersion in water," I read. "Separation is a natural element of the process of decomposition."

He's decomposed?

He might not actually be dead.

Like a zombie?

Like Elvis.

Wouldn't Elvis be like a hundred? Jenny steals a sip of my latte and I can tell she wants to return to her agenda. She stares out the window and taps an appropriate twenty seconds with her finger on the table before asking, But if my guy is single, why would he wear any ring on his ring finger?

Maybe all his other fingers are too fat.

You think I shouldn't see him?

What would you get out of it?

Sex.

Vibrator?

The smell of a man.

Hard to replicate.

The smell of an asshole.

Do assholes smell better than nice guys? I look behind my shoulder to make sure the Scandinavian-looking couple isn't within earshot, on account of all the swearing and sexy talk and them being all white and sweet-tidy-clean Belle-and-Sebastian listening boppity-boop.

You went straight from the cradle to Nik, eh?

I had sex with the first guy I kissed in middle school. Ewen Moss. We were playing seven minutes in heaven. Had an abortion. After that I stopped shaving my pits and showering. Then I came to Edmonton and met Nik.

Damn, Sara. The seven minutes weren't for intercourse.

When were we supposed to say no?

You were supposed to let him unzip your jeans and get maybe three fingers in and then giggle all high-pitched until he stopped. You had no girlfriends?

There was this girl Rita. She had an overbite like Freddie Mercury but not his bone structure. Or stage presence. No guy would go near her.

Jenny picks up her plate and licks the crumbs off it.

I bet you had lots of friends, I say.

Nope. I was the mysterious slutty chick with a thirty-year-old boyfriend.

I was the mysterious slutty chick who'd only had sex once.

Those high-school boys were so afraid of us.

I give Jenny a high-five and ask if she thinks Nik is a nice guy or an asshole.

Nice guy, of course. But not quite flaccid.

I nod. I can't tell Jenny about the baristas. It seems so stupid. The father of her child was fucking dish pigettes under her nose before she even went into labour. But at least he was honest about it. And Jenny's my girl. I want to tell her about how Nik wears skid-marked sweats to bed now and how when I'm in my sex panties and I bend down to pet the cat and I look through the nook in my armpit he's not spying my ass, he's checking his phone for hockey scores or craft beer reviews. And about how, when we do make love and I take off my shirt, he lowers his eyes and hands to my hips to avoid addressing how even tits so small as mine could droop. And about how once I've had one hairy ball in my mouth after the other and I spread his legs farther and run the tip of my tongue down till I feel him taut and tangy, he clenches up and pushes my head away and says he's not sure he wiped properly. And I want to ask her what to do. What do you do when you meet this guy when you're eighteen who seems quirky and cool and wears mismatched socks and peels Bosc pears for you and marks you like a dog with his saliva and then he turns into this slick-haired, finger-gun-shooting, small-talk spewer who reserves his dwindling stores of kindness for a bunch of coffee-slinging angels of darkness who are young enough to befriend his daughter and are only kind to him in return because they're paid to provide superior customer service? What do you do with a crumb-by-crumb betrayal you only notice once there's not enough good left to spread the jam on?

But Jenny's idea of commitment is using the same shade of lipstick until the tube runs out, and she has yet to accomplish this. She's holding her hands together in that namaste way, telling me how nice-guy Nik is. How he makes those killer chicken wings and not too spicy the way most men would. How he coaches my daughter's softball team and how he looks at me in the same way he looks at our daughter. Proud and admiring and kind of worried. And this makes me cry, with my palms to my eyes and hunched over my latte. And Jenny says, Oh shit, your dad. But it's so much bigger than that.

Why are you avoiding Nik? Jenny asks.

I shake my head.

Jenny waits for something to come out of my mouth and then finally says, Okay. She reaches out and presses her key into my palm. She says, I gotta get to work. Stay at my place as long as you want. The kid's with his dad this week, so you can walk around in your panties and stuff.

Jenny turns to leave, then lunges back. That's my only key, so wear it around your neck.

When Jenny walks away, she pulls my life force with her, like a tide. I should have a reason to walk briskly from point A to B like she does, like all the people outside do. But I bet they all had fathers. Fathers who taught them to change a tire and growled at their boyfriends and gave them away to their husbands named Brad who are child psychologists or school principals and make them bulgur pilaf on Sundays and drive them to the lake in summer and otherwise bask with them in their normal, normal lives.

The Scandinavian-looking couple touch hips while one works the till and the other the espresso machine. The wife lets the husband go on about ideal brew time and doesn't roll her eyes when he dumps an espresso because it took thirty-one seconds to pull rather than the desired twenty to thirty. She doesn't joke that it's better too long than premature. Perhaps I've not chosen the most fitting coffee shop to patronize after all.

It's Monday, which means it's Margarita Monday at Julio's Barrio, and I am to meet Jenny here after work. I hope she won't show up with Some of the Girls—her fellow office assistants with last-name first names like Mackenzie and Argyle who nibble at plain corn chips like field mice and don't order guacamole but eye me desperately and mumble dieting mantras while I eat mine. They drink tequila straight up because it has fewer calories that way and, after half an hour's passed, holler about Mike from accounting's tight pants and that time Kennedy ass-fucked Paul from marketing with a green highlighter, mistakenly using Elmer's rubber cement as lube, at the Legendary Office Christmas Party of 2019.

I'm under the Trump piñata, which is the most coveted seat in the joint. When a jumbo plate of nachos is ordered on Margarita Monday, the cooks play "The Mexican Hat Dance" and everyone bashes at Trump with replicas of fence posts from The Donald Trump Great Great Huge Wall of Mexico™ for the duration of the song. If there's a breach in the papier-mâché, Donald spews gold-foiled chocolate coins, Cherry Bombers, canisters of orange spray-tan, nacho-grade tear gas, Nancy Pelosi action figures, faux squirrel skins, and pink toques for all. The last time I saw Trump burst was at Nik's fortieth birthday party five months ago. I jabbed the bat between Donald's eyes and tore at him down to his bullfrog chin. Nik tipped his head to the ceiling and I popped Cherry Bombers down his throat. Nik held me with all his fingers entwined around my waist, exposed his cherry-red teeth, and said, You are vicious and sublime. I told him he looked like a happy cannibal grabbing me so with his blood-red mouth. Any other time I would've bitten my tongue. He would've made some remark about a man's necessity for flesh and was there no respite from the vegan police with me around. But that night he tightened his grip and bit my neck. He took me home and fucked me like every inch of my body was a welcome surprise, like my every unconventionality was beautiful simply because it was mine. Then we woke up and he was forty. And he was not Don Draper or Jason Seaver or even George Jetson. He pierced his failings with metal hooks and hung them from my limbs, and I became weighted and precarious with his discontent.

Jenny won't be here for another hour, and my only entertainment is a window to Whyte Avenue. There's a girl with turquoise hair outside. It's short and juts from her scalp in felted clusters. She's painted her eyes glimmery peach all around. It brings out the red in her eyeballs, makes her look like a lab bunny—but in a good way. She's with this guy with a kempt beard and dark toque wearing coveralls ironically. Honestly, show me a clean-shaven man without a lid and I'll cream my panties. His jaw waggles and he slices the air between them, fingers stitched together like patronizing soldiers as he mansplains Tarkovsky's use of recurrent imagery or perhaps why he believes her DivaCup is more harmful to the environment than tampons. That annoying voice in my head asks why I assume all men are dicks. Maybe he's pinpointing his areas of vulnerability with those shark-fin fingers.

I'm on my third margarita and Donald's looking more and more like a constipated orangutan swaying above my head when Jenny's giggle wafts in. She's accompanied by a pant-suited posse clicking toward me in five-inch heels. Argyle, Quinn, Emerson, and some dude. They're all huddled, faces in, sweeping the bar like a tornado. I duck and run, tell the host they'll cover my bill, and escape out the back door. Quinn is the youngest OA at Jenny's work, fresh out of secretary school—an institution I thought had died with second-wave feminism. She's always touching my clothes and telling me how "retro" I look. Last time Jenny brought her out, Quinn told me she hopes she looks as good as me when she's old.

It's November freezing outside. Head in the refrigerator cold. Not the best day to leave the house—for good—in a jean jacket and macramé scarf. The Edmontonians are huddled into their collars like frigid turtles, unaware of one another, not yet over October's on-again off-again above-zero seductions, holding out for one more hit before December. I look for Nik's slick of black hair tucked into a pilling green wool overcoat, the slowly unravelling scarf I knitted but never finished for him on the seventh anniversary of my landing on his doorstep. The seventh is wool. He's not on the street. He's not inside his coffee shop. I press my face into the glass and wish for his presence. My dad died, I want to yell at him, and here you are. I want him to be as awful as I imagine him to be. To live up to my fear he won't return home at the end of each day. Because the alternative—the stripping off layers of yourself and feeding them to another like slices of prosciutto—feels infinitely more dangerous than solitude.

My tiny bladder leads me to tug at the coffee shop's door, but they're closed for the night and the little Groke mopping the floor inside only shrugs at me. At Jenny's place, I pee and try a few of her prescription drugs. I spend far too much time searching for her son's diary. He's normally home when I visit—a greasy toad crumpled into his gaming remote on Jenny's plaid vintage recliner. Jenny uses the word *vintage* to describe anything she found on the side of the road. How could I not take this opportunity to venture into his bedroom? This room's brand of funk is a mixture of rancid butter, rotten eggs, and cloves. Cloves? No, mould. There is no diary to be found, but atop a pile of dirty track pants is a Captain's Log-style notebook that deciphers butt days from abs days. He must be like Nik, with a little man inside his head who remembers everything perfectly, as it happened, including every feeling he did not feel. Under Jenny's son's mattress next to the obligatory crusty sock is a stash of *Hustler* mags from the seventies he must've inherited from his on-again off-again father. I haven't passed anything down to my daughter, other than the mole under my left armpit, and neither of us knows what to do with that. We exist on different planets. If only we could gawk at a nice set of jugs and make magazines sticky together. What if she thinks of me the way I thought of my mother? What if my mother thought of me the way I think of my daughter? I take the *Hustler*s to the bathroom, run a bath, and mix in all of Jenny's bubble flavours, from Sugar Plum Fairy to Grandma's Rose Garden. I spend quite some time practising the *Hustler* ladies' frog-legged, archy-backed, under the nipple boob-cupping, jaw-dropped, bottom-half-of-two-front-teeth-exposed poses in the bathroom mirror. I trim my pubes accordingly with Jenny's bang scissors. I lie in the bath, make bubble arm rests and pretend I'm Dr. Claw. I make bubble clouds and play Care Bears with Jenny's scrappy bits of soap. I lie very still and soak up all the hot until it's gone, then add more, and repeat and repeat. It's been so long since I've become pruney in the bath.

When I hear Jenny's drunken soft-whispered drawl and a low voice enter the apartment, the most important thing to take care of before I'm discovered seems to be wiping my stray hairs off her scissors, the bathroom floor, the toilet seat. Jenny puts on her Beach House playlist, which means she's in for some serious panties-on couch action. If it was a panties-off night, she'd go for something less morose-'n-dreamy and more sexy-fun, like a few of Grimes's higher-pitched, breathy numbers on repeat. I think I'll be safe here in the bathroom, corpselike in the tub, until Jenny and dude finish pressing hard parts against soft parts and grabbing at the bits of each other's bare skin that become exposed during said pressing.

Until he says, I should go, and she says, Yeah, you should, and then bites his bottom lip one more time, and he says, Jeeeenny, in that you-naughty-naughty-girl voice.

We always think we're safe, don't we, until somebody needs to pee.

Jenny stumbles into the bathroom, twirls against the toilet, grabs the tub edge, then makes eye contact with me through the foam. Jesus, Sara, she says, then she covers her mouth and spurt-laughs into her hand. She takes off her bra and panties, which was all she had on, and climbs in with me.

What about the dude? I whisper.

He can wait.

Is it the married guy?

Jenny nods.

Is he married?

Jenny nods and adds, But unhappily.

Who isn't?

Jenny holds my jaw with both of her hands and stares into my eyes. Are you okay?

I took some pills. I hold Jenny's wrists and say, I'm so good.

My antibiotics? You're hilarious.

I press my face into her chest, but the top part, so my chin rests on her boob. Men must like women who have actual boobs, I say.

I love your little bee stings. Jenny rubs a thumb over one of my nipples. I part my lips into her skin. It tastes like buttered flowers. Would it be so difficult for Nik to moisturize?

Didn't you need to pee? I ask.

Already did.

I thought it got warmer.

Why'd you run out of the bar?

I don't know. Your work friends.

Jenny's hand is on my waist now, and she squeezes me like she's ripping apart a baguette. He won't fuck me, she says.

The wife?

If his penis doesn't cheat, he doesn't cheat.

I slide into Jenny and wrap my legs around her waist easy and slippy under the water. She licks my throat and I grab her ribs, each finger finds a little gap to fit into. I tilt my pelvis into her. Jenny grabs my bum and pulls me close. I bite her neck and cup one of her boobs. It feels weird to hold a boob from this side of things. Jenny runs two fingers between my bum cheeks. I press myself in and away from her soft belly and suck and suck at her neck. She mewls like a kitten, but a bit too loud. Is she here to score girl-on-girl sexy points with Married Dude?

Jenny? Is someone there? he says, and I hear the squeak of the vintage recliner.

All good, she yells. Be right out.

We should be together, I say.

We'd drive each other crazy, Jenny says.

I guess. You're so self-centred.

You're so high maintenance.

I curl my back away from Jenny and wrap myself into a ball. Really?

You think everyone's out to hurt you.

Everyone does hurt me.

You get so close. Jenny rests her elbow on the tub edge and laces her fingers together. You feel betrayed if I change my hair without you.

That one time, I say. I wanted pink hair too.

I take a deep breath and blow a canyon into my bubbles. I tell Jenny, I thought my dad would come back and save me some day. But this is my life.

Maybe he only lost a foot at sea. Maybe he's a pirate.

He used to call me Jellybean. But the day he left, Sara. I should've stopped him.

He would've left some other day.

Nik hasn't spoken my name in months.

He would've left by now.

He has these baristas.

At least he's not—Jenny wags her thumb toward the bathroom door. He probably thinks I'm massively constipated.

Blame your period.

Jenny wraps herself in a towel and goes out like that, leaving her bra and panties like snotty tissues under a sick bed. I hear her say goodnight to Married Dude. I hear her say she likes spending time with him and I hear him say, This was fun. I hear him tell her she's cute and sexy, but he never says beautiful. I hear him tell her to take good care and to keep in touch and then I hear Jenny's door close. I hear Jenny repeat, slow and soft, Keep. In. Touch. I leave the bathroom wrapped in a towel of my own. I lean into her from the back, skin to skin, terry to terry. I rest my lips on her shoulder and hold her hand.

Jenny and I sleep in her bed with our underwear on. She twists around me and falls asleep squeezing me like I don't require oxygen. Nik in bed behind me is long and lean and elastic, like a whisk. I miss his fingers between my thighs and the smell of his bedtime breath. Toothpaste mint overcome by pruney mouth. I will return home for breakfast tomorrow. I'll sit between my daughter and Nik at the kitchen table. My daughter will say, Where'd you come from? and Nik will put a bagel in the toaster for me without asking where I was, without saying anything. I'll wait for the right time to tell him about my dad, like that night, during a commercial break when the Oilers have just scored, as Nik rides their momentum, able to morph elation into sympathy. He'll look into my eyes and tell me he's sorry. And not only for the loss of my dad. Nik will be sorry for every time I've lost him—to his insular worries, to his misplaced ambition, to all the twenty-five-year-old girls he's wanted to absorb his shame. I'll look him back in the eye and I'll thank him. And I will be thankful for his sympathy and his remorse, but most of all for the beat he waits, once the Oilers are back on the ice, before reverting his eyes to the TV.

DAVID HUEBERT

CHEMICAL VALLEY

kneel down and reach for the nearest bird, hydraulics buzzing in my teeth and knees. The pigeon doesn't flinch or blink. No blood. No burn-smell. Sal's there in seconds, his face a blear of night-shift grog. He rubs his bigger eye, squats by the carcasses. Behind him the river wends and glimmers, slicks through the glare of sixty-two refineries.

Sal thumbs his coverall pockets. "Poison, you figure?"

"Leak maybe."

Suzy appears next to Sal, seeping chew-spit into her Coke can. She leans over and takes a pigeon in her Kevlared paw. Brings it to her face. "Freaky," she says, bottom lip bulging. "Eyes still open." She wiggles her rat-face into a grin, a frond of tobacco wagging in her bottom teeth.

I can't afford to say it: "Saving that for later?"

Suzy flares: "What?"

"The chew."

Suzy puts a hand over her mouth, speaks with taut lips: "Enough of your guff."

I snort. "Guff?"

She sets the bird down, hitches her coveralls. Lips closed, she tongues the tobacco loose and swallows. "Clean 'em up," she says, nodding at the pigeons. She spins and walks away, a slurry of chew-spit mapping her path across the unit.

What you might find, if you were handling a dead pigeon, is something unexpected in the glassy cosmos of its eye: a dark beauty, a molten alchemy. You might find a pigeon's iris looks how you imagine the Earth's core—pebble-glass waves of crimson, a perfect still shudder of rose and lilac. What you might do, if you were placing a dead pigeon into the incinerator, is take off your Kevlar glove and touch your bare index finger to its cornea. What you might do before dropping the bird into a white-hot Mordor of carbon and coke is touch your fingertip to that unblinking membrane and hold it there, feeling a mangle of tenderness and violation, thinking this may be the loveliest secret you have ever touched.

I'm telling Eileen how I want to be buried, namely inside a tree. We're sitting in bed eating Thai from the mall and listening to the 6 p.m. construction outside our window—the city tearing up the whole street along with tree roots and a rusted tangle of lead pipes—and I'm telling Eileen it's called a biodegradable burial pod. Mouth full of cashew curry and I'm saying what they do is put your remains in this egg-looking thing like the xenomorph's cocoon from *Alien: Resurrection* but it's made of biodegradable plastic. I'm telling Eileen it's called "capsula mundi" and what they do is hitch the remains to a semi-mature tree and plant the whole package.

Stuff you down in fetal position and let you gradually decay until you become nitrogen, seep into soil.

Chewing panang, Eileen asks where I got the idea about the burial pod and I tell her Facebook or maybe an email newsletter. "You click on that shit? Why are you even thinking about this now? You just turned thirty-four."

I don't tell her about the basement, about Mum. I don't tell her about the pigeons strewn out on the concrete and then going supernova in the incinerator and it gets you thinking about flesh, about bodies, about waste. I don't tell her about Blane, the twenty-nine-year-old long-distance runner who got a heart attack sitting at the panel in the Alkylation unit. Blane didn't die but he did have to get surgery and a pacemaker and that sort of thing gets you thinking. Which is how you end up lying in bed at night checking your pulse and feeling like your chest is shrinking and thinking about the margin of irregular and erratic.

Picking a bamboo shoot from her teeth: "Since when are you into trees?"

She says it smug. She says it like Ms. University Sciences and nobody else is allowed to like trees. I don't tell her how we're all compost and yes I read that on a Facebook link. I also do not tell her about the article's tagline: "Your carbon footprint doesn't end in the grave." Reaching for the pad thai, I tell her about the balance, how it's only natural. How the human body's rich in nitrogen, how when you use a coffin there's a lot of waste because the body just rots on its own when it could be giving nutrients to the system. Not to mention all the metals and treated woods in coffins. I tell her how the idea is to phase out traditional graveyards entirely, replace them with grave-forests.

"Hmm," Eileen says, gazing out the window—the sky a caramelized rose. "Is this a guilt thing, from working at the plants?"

I tell her no, maybe, I don't know. An excavator hisses its load into the earth.

"Is this why you were so weird about your mother's funeral?"

I ask what she means and she says never mind, sorry.

"Do you ever imagine they're ducks?"

Eileen asks what and I tell her the loaders and the bulldozers and the cranes. Sometimes I imagine they're wildlife, ducks or geese. And maybe why they're crying like that is because they're in distress. Like maybe they've lost their eggs and all they want is to get them back and when you think about it like that it's still bad but at least it's not just machines screaming and blaring because they're tearing up old sidewalks to put new ones down.

"Ducks," Eileen says. "Probably still be one working for every three scratching their guts for overtime pay."

She stacks the containers and reaches for the vaporizer on the nightstand, asking if I love trees so much why didn't I become a landscaper or a botanist or an arborist. I shrug, not mentioning the debt or the mortgage or the pharmaceutical bills. Not mentioning that if I wanted to do something it would be the comics store but there's no market in Sarnia anyway.

I tell her it's probably too late for a career change.

"No," she coos, pinching my chin the way I secretly loathe. She smiles her sweet stoned smile, a wisp of non-smoke snaking through her molars. "You could do anything. You could be so much." Eileen lies down on her back on the bed, telling the ceiling I could be so much and the worst part is she means it.

The worst and the best all coiled together as I reach out and thumb the curry sauce from her chin.

Eileen tells me she needs the bathroom so I help her out of bed and into her chair. I stand outside the bathroom door listening to the faucet's gentle gush and thinking about later, when Eileen falls asleep and I drift down to the basement, to Mum.

In 1971 the Trudeau government issued a ten-dollar bill picturing Sarnia's Chemical Valley as a paean to Canadian progress. Inked in regal purple, the buildings rise up space-aged and triumphant, a *Jetsons* wet dream. Towers slink up to the sky and cloudlike drums pepper the ground, a suspended rail line curling through the scene. Smokestacks and ladders and tanks and tubs. Glimmering steel and perfect concrete, a shimmering fairy city, and the strange thing is that what you don't see is oil, what you never see is oil. The other strange thing is that this is how Sarnia used to be seen, that not so long ago the plants were shiny and dazzling and now they're rusty with paint peeling off the drums and poor safety and regular leaks and weeds all over, stitching concrete seams.

On the drive to work a woman on the radio is talking about birth rates as the cornfields whish and whisper. Eileen doesn't know this or need to, but I drive the long way to work because I like to drive through the cornfields. What I like about them is the sameness: corn and corn and corn and it makes you think that something is stable, stable and alive and endless, or about as close as you can get. If Eileen was in the car she'd say, "As high as an elephant's eye in July." Then she'd probably say her thing about ethanol. How the nitrogen fertilizer comes from ammonia, which comes from natural gas. How the petrochemical fertilizer is necessary to grow super huge varieties of hybrid corn products that mostly turn into livestock feed but also a significant portion turns into ethanol. Ethanol that is then used as a biofuel supplement to gasoline so what it is is this whole huge cycle of petroleum running subterranean through modern biological life.

On the radio they're saying how first it was the birds and then it was the reserve and now they're getting worried. Now they're seeing plant workers, especially the women, producing only female children. No official studies on the area because Health Canada won't fund them, but the anecdotal evidence is mounting and mounting and the whole community knows it's in their bodies, in their intimate organs, zinging through their spit and blood and lymph nodes.

"Hey," Suzy says, slurring chew-spit into her Coke can. "What do you call a Mexican woman with seven kids?" I try to shrug away the punch line, but Sal gives his big-lipped smirk and asks what. "Consuelo," Suzy says, her mouth a snarl of glee. She puts her hand down between her knees and mimes a pendulum.

I smile in a way that I guess is not convincing because Suzy says, "What's the matter Jerr-Bear?" I tell her it's not funny.

"Fuck you it isn't."

"Think I'll do my geographics."

"You do that," Suzy says, turning back to Sal. "Can't leave you here with Pockets all shift." "Pockets" being what Suzy calls me in her kinder moments, when she doesn't feel like calling me

"Smartass" or "Thesaurus" or "Mama's boy." Something to do with I guess putting my hands in my coverall pockets too much.

I walk away while Sal starts saying something about Donaldson or Bautista and Suzy makes her usual joke about me and the Maglite.

Before she got sick, Eileen used to work in research, and on slow days that is most days I used to think up toward her. I'd look up toward the shiny glass windows of the research building and think of Eileen working on the other side. Mostly what they do up there is ergonomic self-assessments and loss prevention self-assessments but sometimes they do cutting and cracking. A lot of what they do is sit up there staring at glove matrices and gauges and screens, but I'd always picture Eileen with her hands in the biosafety cabinet. I'd picture her in goggles and full face mask and fire-retardant suit, reaching through the little window to mix the catalyst in and then watching the crude react in the microscope. Because when Eileen was working she loved precision and she loved getting it right but most of all she loved watching the oil split and change and mutate. Say what you want about oil but the way Eileen described it she always made it seem beautiful: dense and thick, a million different shades of black. She used to say how the strange thing with the oil is that if you trace it back far enough you see that it's life, that all this hydrocarbon used to be vegetables and minerals and zooplankton. Organisms that got caught down there in some cavern where they've been stewing for five hundred million years. How strange it is to look out at this petroleum Xanadu and think that all the unseen sludge running through it was life, once—that it was all compost, all along.

In 2003 there was a blackout all across Ontario and the north-eastern United States. A blackout caused by a software bug and what happened was people could see the stars again from cities. In dense urban areas the Milky Way was suddenly visible again, streaming through the unplugged vast. What also happened was babies, nine months later a horde of blackout babies, the hospitals overwhelmed with newborns because what else do you do when the power goes down. But if you lived in Sarnia what you would remember is the plants. It was nighttime when the power went out and what happened was an emergency shutdown of all systems, meaning all the tail gas burning at once. So every flare from all sixty-two refineries began shooting off together, a tail gas Disneyland shimmering through the river-limned night.

The day shift crawls along. QC QC QC. The highlight is a funny-sounding line we fix by increasing the backpressure. Delivery trucks roll in and out. The pigeons coo and shit and garble in their roosts in the stacks. Freighters park at the dock and pump the tanks full of bitumen—the oil moving, as always, in secret, shrouded behind cylindrical veils of carbon steel. Engineers cruise through tapping iPads, printing the readings from Suzy's board. Swarms of contractors pass by. I stick a cold water bottle in each pocket, which is nice for ten minutes then means I'm carrying piss-warm water around the unit. I do my geographic checks, walk around the tower turning the odd valve when Suzy radios, watch the river rush and kick by the great hulls of the freighters. I think about leaping onto the back of one of those freighters, letting it drag me down the St. Clair and into Erie just to feel the lick of breeze on neck.

Time sags and sags and yawns. By 10 a.m. I can feel the sun howling off the concrete, rising up vengeful and gummy. Doesn't matter that there's a heat warning, you've still got to wear your coveralls and your steel toes and your hardhat, the sweat gooing up the insides of your arms, licking the backs of your knees. The heat warning means we take "precautions." It means coolers full of Nestle water sweating beside the board. It means we walk slowly around the unit. As slow as we can possibly move but the slow walking becomes its own challenge because the work's still got to get done.

The river gets me through the shift: the curl and cool of it, its great improbable blue. The cosmic-bright blue that's supposedly caused by the zebra mussels the government put all over Ontario to make the water blue and pretty but if Eileen were here she'd say her thing about the algae. How she learned in first-year bio that what the zebra mussels do is eat all the particles from the lake, allowing room for algae to grow beyond their boundaries and leading to massive poisonous algae blooms in Lake Huron and Lake Erie. So you think you're fixing something, but really there's no fixing and how fitting that one way or another the river's livid blue is both beautiful and polluted, toxic and sublime.

"Heard about those bodies?" Sal asks, thumbing through his phone as I pass by the board. I ask what bodies and he says the ones in Toronto. "Like a half dozen of them, some kind of landscaper-murderer stashing bodies in planters all over the city."

I kill the shift as usual: walk around wiggling the flashlight thinking about the different spots in the river and diving into them with my mind. Thinking about what might be sleeping down there—maybe a pike or a smelt or a rainbow trout nestled among the algae and the old glass Coke bottles. Sometimes I think my way across the bridge, over to Port Huron. Wonder if there's an operator over there doing the same thing, thinking back across the river toward me.

I drive home the long way, which means cornfields and wind turbines in the distance as the sky steeps orange pekoe. In the rear-view a flare shoots up from the plants. Getting closer, I pass through a gauntlet of turbines, feeling them more than I see them. Carbon filament sentries. Once, I passed an enormous truck carrying a wind turbine blade and at first I thought it was a whale. It reminded me of videos I'd seen of Korean authorities transporting a sperm whale bloated with methane, belching its guts across the tarmac. The truck had a convoy and a bunch of orange WIDE LOAD signs and I passed it slowly, partly because of the danger and partly because there was a pulse to it, something drawing me in. The great sleek curve of the blade, its unreal whiteness.

Eileen's still up, vaping in her chair by the window. "Sorry," she says, spinning her chair to look at me. "Couldn't sleep." I tell her she can vape in the kitchen or wherever she likes but she looks at me with her stoned slanting smile and tells me it's not that. Says how she's been looking out into the yard a lot and when she does it she thinks about the teenagers. She looks at me like she wants me to ask for details. I don't, but she continues anyway. Rehearses how those kids in the seventies got trapped in the abandoned fallout shelter. "You know, the yards were so long because the properties used to be cottages and the old shelter was overgrown and the teens were skipping school and smoking up and the excavator came through and started to fill it in and no one realized the teens were missing until days later. The only explanation was that they were scared, so scared of getting caught that they stayed quiet, let it happen, hoped it would pass."

"You don't believe all that do you?"

Eileen shrugs, still staring out the window. "No. Maybe. I just like the story."

I ask how's the pain today and she says manageable. Turns her face toward me but doesn't meet my eyes. I ask her out of ten and she says you know I hate that. She asks is something wrong and I tell her no. "Something you're not telling me about?" I don't respond and she doesn't push it.

We watch the original *Total Recall* and when we get to the part with the three-breasted woman Eileen asks if I find that strange or sexy and I tell her neither, or both. Eventually Eileen drifts off but when I stand up she lurches awake. She asks where I'm going and I say just downstairs to read the new *Deadpool* unless she wants the bedside lamp on. She says no, asks when I'm coming to bed. I tell her soon and she says cuddle me when you get here. "Don't just lie there," she says. "Hold me." I tell her yes, of course, and head down to the sweet dank sogg of the basement.

Mum listens with tender quiet as I tell her about my day— about Suzy, about the pigeons, about the construction. Mum is gentle and sweet, her gold incisor catching light from the bare pull-string bulb. Eventually I check my phone and see that it's pushing eleven and I should probably head upstairs if I want my six to seven hours. I give Mum a goodnight kiss and tell her to get some rest and then I notice something strange in the floor, stoop down to inspect.

A hand-shaped imprint in the foundation floor.

Mum looks on, her face a void, as I toe that dark patch with my basement-blackened sock and find that it's wet, sodden. The hole's a bit sandy and when I get closer I smell it. Muskeg. Raw Lambton skunk.

I prod a little deeper and become a stranger, become someone who would stick a curious thumb into such a cavity. The oil comes out gooey and black and smelling sharp, a little sulphurous.

I dream of bodies, the ones buried in planters in Toronto. The ones I'd heard about on the radio—this killer targeting gay men in Toronto and the more planters they dug up the more bodies they found. In the dream the bodies aren't skeletons, not yet. They're in the active decay stage: their organs starting to liquify, the soft tissue browning and breaking down while the hair, teeth, and bone remain intact. I see them crawling up from planters all across the city. Not vengeful or anything. Just digging, rising, trying to get back.

"Would you have liked to become an engineer?" We're in the bug tent sipping iced tea and listening to a sweet chorus of loaders and bulldozers, the air heady with the lilt of tar.

"I am one. A chemical engineer." I can see Eileen wanting to laugh and fighting it. Not like I've got any delusions about my four-year Lambton College diploma, but technically it is a credential in chemical engineering.

"Maybe an urban planner," Eileen says. "Have you heard about all this stuff they're doing in cities now? Condos with elevators big enough for cars. Cute little electric cars that you'll bring right up to your apartment with you."

"Sounds more like an Eileen thing."

A bird lands in the armpit of the oak. A pocket-sized black-bird with a slash of red on its wing. The one I love but can never remember its name.

Eileen sips her tea and says yeah I'm probably right but it's just she can tell the hours are getting to me. The hours and the nights and the overtime. She reminds me how I told her, once, that it's like a sickness, the overtime. "You could do whatever you want," she says. "You could be so much."

The worst part is she always means it and the worst part is it's not true. Not true because Mum worked part-time and Dad died so young that there was no money for me to do anything but CPET. I don't tell her because she already knows about the comics store, about how maybe I could write one on the side and I already have the character—BioMe, the scientist turned mutant tree-man after attempting to splice photo-synthesis into the human genome.

"You're so creative, you could be so much. Like your comics store idea. And remember that musical you wrote in high school, *Hydrocarbonia*?" She chuckles. "There was that three-eyed coyote and the plant worker Village People chorus?"

"I think it was basically a *Simpsons* rip-off. Mr. Hunter went with *Guys and Dolls*."

"Still. You're a poet at heart."

"The bard of bitumen."

"What I mean is I love you but sometimes I feel like all you do is work and all I do is sleep and we never see each other and I just wish we had something else, something more."

A quick haze of stupidity in which I contemplate telling her about Mum.

Then I see a seagull in the distance, watch as it catches a thermal and rides high and higher, an albatross floating through the glazed crantini sky.

"One more shift," I tell her. "Then four off."

She doesn't need to roll her eyes. "Look," she says, pointing up at the oak. "A red-winged blackbird."

On the drive to work they're saying about the fish. Saying about the drinking water downstream, in Windsor and Michigan. Saying about the tritium spilling into Lake Huron. You think Chernobyl and you think Blinky the three-eyed fish, but what you don't think is an hour north or so, where Bruce Power leaks barrels of radioactive tritium into Lake Huron. They're saying how significant quantities of anti-depressants have been found in fish brains in the Great Lakes.

I drive past the rusting drums and have to stop for a moment because there are some protesters forming a drum circle. They're holding signs that read "STOP LINE 9" and chanting about stolen Native land and of course they're right but I don't smile or stop or acknowledge them. Just park and walk through security, a new sting in the awful.

Ways people deal with constant low-level dread: the myth that the wind blows the fumes south, toward Aamjiwnaang, toward Corunna, toward Walpole. That the airborne toxicity lands ten kilometres to the south. That the people who live north of the plants won't get sick or at least not as sick. As if wind could really dilute the impact of living beside a cluster of sixty-two petrochemical refineries that never sleep, could change the fact that you live in a city where Pearl Harbor–style sirens sound their test alarm every Monday at 12:30 to remind you that leaks could happen at any moment. There's a joke around Streamline, a joke that is not a joke: the retirement package is great if you make it to fifty-five. Which is not inaccurate in my family seeing as Dad went at fifty-two and Mum followed at fifty-six and they said the lung cancer had nothing to do with the plants and the brain cancer had nothing to do with Mum's daily swims from the bridge to Canatara Beach. The strange pride among people who work the plants: A spending your oil salary on Hummers and motorcycles and vacations to Cuban beaches with plastic cups kind of pride. A live rich live hard kind of pride. The yippee ki-yay of knowing that Sarnia is the leukemia capital of Canada and the brain cancer capital of Canada and the air pollution capital of Canada but also knowing that oil is what you know and what your parents knew and all your family's in Lambton County so what else are you going to do but stay.

We're putting on our face masks and backpacks while Don the safety protocol officer explains for the hundredth time about the new model of self-contained breathing apparatus and the new standard-issue Kevlar gloves. Telling us once again that personal safety is paramount even though all of us know that what operators are here for is to control situations.

I'm sitting there watching sailboats tack their way across the lake while Don goes on about the hydrogen sulfide incident that happened two years ago. Incident meaning leak. Telling us again how the thing about hydrogen sulfide is that you can't see it, so you can't actually see or smell when it's on fire. Two years ago when a vehicle melted in the loading dock. An invisible sulfide fire came through and before the operators could shut it down the truck in the loading bay just melted. The tires evaporated and the air hissed out of them and the whole truck sank to the floor, a puddle of melted paint on the concrete and nothing left of the truck but a gleaming skeleton of carbon steel.

We used to swim in the lake at night, just the two of us. Dad was usually home watching the Blue Jays so me and Mum would drive up to a secret little beach in the north and we'd swim out into the middle of the river where the lights from Port Huron gleamed and wiggled in the darkness. Sometimes it would rain and the rain would make the water warmer than the air. I'd seen a water snake at the beach once and I always imagined them down there among our legs. Though Mum had assured me they were non-venomous, I saw them sharp-toothed and cunning, biding their time. Sometimes Mum would dip down below the water, her head disappearing for what seemed an impossibly long time, and I don't know how she found me but she'd wrangle her arms around both my legs and pin me for a moment while I kicked and bucked and then we'd both come up gasping and squealing and giggling in the black water, a gelatin dazzle of refinery lights.

"So what tree?" Eileen asks, watching the sun bleed pink delirium over the abandoned Libcor refinery. Eileen in her chair and the van parked behind us. In front, the overgrown refinery that shut down thirty years ago after a mercaptan leak. When they left, the company kept the lot. Took down all the tall buildings and left a waste of concrete with a railway running through it, surrounded by a barbed-wire fence.

I ask for clarification and Eileen asks what tree I'd want to be buried in and I pause to think about it, looking out over the crabgrass and goldenrod and firepits full of scorched goldenrod. "Think there are any animals in there?"

Eileen says yeah, probably, like Chernobyl. She knows about Chernobyl from a documentary. In the Exclusion Zone, there's a place called the Red Forest. It's a bit stunted and the trees have a strange ginger hue but the wildlife is thriving— boar, deer, wolves, eagles. Eileen says how nuclear radiation might actually be better for animals than human habitation.

I stand quietly, holding Eileen's chair and watching the sun pulse and glow and vanish. She reaches back and takes my hand, rubs the valleys between my fingers. Eventually, without saying anything, we turn for the van.

"You ever think about concrete?" Eileen asks as I'm fastening her chair into the van. "How it seems so permanent. How it's all around us and we walk and drive on it believing it's hard and firm and solid as the liquid rock it is but really it's nothing like rock at all. Weeds and soil beneath it and all of it ready to rise up at the gentlest invitation. It's very fragile, very temporary."

On the way home we pass by the rubber plant and the abandoned Blue Water Village and beyond it Aamjiwnaang and Eileen says, "Incredible shrinking territory." The reserve used to stretch from Detroit to the Bruce Peninsula before being slowly whittled down through centuries of sketchy land deals.

Eileen's maternal grandmother was Ojibwe and she has three cousins on the reserve and we go over once in a while but mostly her tradition is just to say "incredible shrinking territory" when we drive by.

It comes to me when we drive by a bungalow, spot a clutch of them crawling up from the cleft of the foundation. "Sumac, I guess."

"What?"

I say sumac again and Eileen clues in and says aren't those basically weeds. I tell her no, they can get pretty big and I like the fruit, how they go red in autumn. I like how they're sort of bushy and don't have a prominent trunk. How they're spunky and fierce and unpredictable.

"Sumac." Eileen does her pondering frown. "Noted."

It's dark now and the lights are on in Port Huron, flickering out over the river. Looking out the window, Eileen asks me to tell her again how the county used to be. I hold on to the wheel and steer through the great chandelier and tell it how Mum used to. I say about the plank road and the Iroquois Hotel, how Petrolia was incorporated the very year Canada became a country, so we're basically built on oil. I tell about the gushers in every field, soaring up fifty feet and raining down on the fields, clogging up the river and the lakes until the fisherman in Lake Erie complained about the black grit on the hulls of their boats. I tell about the notorious stench of the Lambton skunk, and about the fires. No railway or fire trucks and so when lightning hit and fire took to the fields they often burned for weeks at a time, a carnage of oil-fire raging through the night.

"Wild," she says. "Can you believe all that's gone now? That whole world."

I don't say it's not gone, just invisible—racing through stacks and columns and broilers. I tell her what a perfect word, "wild."

Eileen goes to bed early so I head down to the damp lull of the basement. The hole is the size of a Frisbee now, and it's starting to stink. Sit on the old plastic-plaid lawn chair and talk to Mum about work, about Suzy, about the fish and the pigeons and the ratio.

There's a long silence. I didn't know the whole thing was getting to me. Didn't know how it was building in me, fierce and rank. I tell Mum I'm worried. Worried I'm going to lose her. Worried about the smell, the rot, the secrets. Worried someone's going to figure it out, maybe talk to the taxidermist. And I can't tell Eileen and what are we going to do, what am I going to do?

Mum sits there and listens sweetly. Then she twinkles her gold incisor toward the muskeg hole and I see something strange, something wrong, something white. So I step closer, grab an old chair leg and stir the muskeg a little and yes it definitely is what I think it is: a small bone that could easily be a piece of a raccoon thigh but could also be a human finger.

I wake up at 5 p.m. and find Eileen making pesto which means it must be a good day. As I'm making a Keurig, she tells me there's another one in the toilet. And once she says it I can hear the splashing. "Sorry," she winces, pouring olive oil on a mound of basil and parm. "I wanted to. Just didn't have the energy." She presses a button on the KitchenAid, makes whirling mayhem of leaf and oil.

I put on my spare Kevlars and head into the bathroom, pull the lid up to find the rat floundering, scrambling, its teeth bared and wet with fresh blood from where it must have bludgeoned itself against the porcelain. The water the colour of rust. The rat keeps trying to run up the side of the toilet, losing its purchase and sliding back down in a mayhem of thrashing legs and sploshing water.

Without quite knowing why, I reach in and pin the rat and squat down to look into its eyes. I guess I want to know what it's like to be a rat. Its head flicks back and forth in rage or terror, never meeting my eyes. Maybe it doesn't know how to.

If I let it go it'll just end up back here, in the toilet, in pain. So I hold its head under the water. Pin it as it thrashes and bucks and wheels its legs, switching its ghost-pink tail. Exhausted, the creature doesn't fight much. More or less lets it happen.

I walk it through a Stonehenge of pylons and descend into the guts of the exhumed city street. I lay the rat in a puddle at the mouth of a culvert and throw some sludge over it. Walk back between a mound of PVC piping and a wrecked Jenga of blasted asphalt.

Back inside, I tell Eileen I released it alive. "Good," she says. "I'm getting tired of this. Must have something to do with the plumbing, the construction."

"Should be over soon."

"What should?"

"Want to go down to the river?"

We park at Point Edward and I wheel Eileen down to the waterfront, where the river curls and snarls and chops its dazzling blue. Underfoot there's a belligerence of goose shit. We watch a pair and Eileen tells me they mate for life and get fierce about their young. They've been known to attack adult humans to protect them. I look at the geese and wonder how long their families have been nesting on this river.

"When did they stop migrating?" Eileen asks.

Which makes me think of a book I read once, where the main character keeps asking where the ducks go in winter. I can't remember what book or what the answer was if there was one. I tell her I don't know and she tells me how weird it is that there's this whole big thing about Canada geese flying south in winter but as far as she can tell they never leave.

"I think it's the northern ones, more so."

"And what, they migrate down here? Winter in scenic Sarnia?"

Beneath the bridge a teenager launches into a backflip. Executes perfectly to uproarious applause. His audience: a chubby redheaded boy and three thin girls in dripping bathing suits. Eileen stops for a moment and I can see her watching them and maybe she's thinking how comfortable they are. How cozy. How nice it must be to just have a body and not think about it.

Above them, transport trucks arc through a highway in the sky.

The four off blurs by in a haze of Domino's and Netflix and assuring Eileen there's no smell from the basement, that it's probably just the construction. Eileen and I watch all of *Jessica Jones* then all of *The Punisher*, listen to the bleats and chirps of loaders and excavators. On Saturday I find a bone like a human elbow joint in the muskeg, another like an eye socket. Rodent hip, I convince myself. Racoon brow. Squirrel bits. More rats.

Then it's Sunday, meaning back to night shift for eight more on. I whiz past cornfields on the way to work when I notice something strange, something I've never spotted. Which makes sense because it's in the very back of the field and it sort of blends in with a little patch of windbreak trees behind it but there it is: a rusted old derrick in the middle of the cornfield. A wrought-iron steeple rising up through the swishing haze like a puncture in time, a throwback to the days of gushers and teamsters, when the fields were choked with oil and fires burned for weeks.

Eileen texts me to say there's still that weird smell in the house and she's pretty sure it's oil or gas. Maybe it's the stove, should she be worried. She's thinking of texting her brother to come check it out. I tell her no, don't text your brother, I'll open the windows when I get home. Which is when I hear the enunciator.

The blare of the Class A and then the radio crunches and Suzy comes on saying there's a few malfunction lights on in Zone 1 and a flare shooting off. "Main concern is FAL-250A. Flow transfer failure could be a big one, let's get on it."

When a Class A sounds, everyone goes. So it's not just us CDU operators scurrying around, it's also Naphtha and Alkylation and Plastics and the unit is full of bodies. Todd puts on an SCBA though nobody's sure why. Derek and Paul smash into each other at full speed on the Tower #1 scaffold causing Suzy to yell, "No fucking running rule still fucking holds." Stan, one of the night engineers, says maybe it could have something to do with the sludge blanket level in the wastewater valve.

Suzy wheels on him. "How the fuck is that?" When Stan

starts to explain she tells him to go back to his craft beer and his *Magic* card tournaments.

Jack tries again: "Backpressure?"

Suzy glares at him, leaking chew-spit onto the floor. Stan walks off muttering something about valve monkeys. Suzy stares at her board and calls orders out while the rest of us scramble around checking valves and lines and readings.

Sal finds the problem: a release valve is down and there's buildup in the main flare. A buildup of hydrocarbon waste in the thirty-six-inch flare where the tail gas should be burning off, which means a lot of flammable gunk and Suzy's board is telling her the flare's going but the flare is not going.

"Looks like a problem with the pilot flame," Sal shouts from halfway up the tower.

"Getting enough oxygen?" Stan shouts back up.

"Should probably call research," Sal says. Suzy says fuck those fucking lab monkeys then moves toward the tower with a gunslinger strut. Grabbing a rag from a maintenance cart, she starts tying it around a plunger. She sets a boot down on the rubber cup and yanks the wooden handle free. Then she climbs up the tower to the first platform. As she's heading up Sal races down and I'm backing off too as Suzy leans back, shouts, "Heads up," and sends the plunger handle arcing toward the mouth of the flare.

The workers scatter—scurrying into the warehouse and the delivery building, hunching behind trucks and the board. I find a dumpster and cling to the back of it. Sal hits the concrete and joins me just in time to watch the plunger arc and arc and land in the maw of the stack.

The air shimmies and buckles.

The flare lights.

Lights and blasts seventy feet into the moon-limned sky. Air swirls and booms and I clutch my chest because I can't breathe.

The dumpster jumps.

The dumpster becomes a toad and leaps ten feet across the floor. The flare lights, a hissing rage of tail gas, a seventy-foot Roman candle stabbing up at the sickle moon.

No one gets hurt. No one gets in trouble. Stan walks away shaking his head along with the ten or twelve operators gathered on the floor. The enunciator goes quiet and Suzy walks down from the stack, brushing off her knees.

Sal looks over at me, muttering something about being too old for these shenanigans. He walks away huffing, pauses to curse toward the dumpster's skid mark, which is longer than a car. Suzy calls me over and tells me I didn't see shit, then tells me to look after the flare for the rest of my shift.

"What do you mean 'look after it'?"

"Stand there and watch it Stephen fucking Hawking."

So I stand there and watch it.

The moon grins down and the flame shoots up beside it for ten minutes, then twenty, with no sign of abating. I pace around Tower #1, checking pressures and temps and turning valves as needed but always keeping that flare in eyeshot.

One hour. Two.

Down by the river I see the lakeshore going liquid and sort of throbbing. At first I think it must be gas. Then I think I must be hallucinating because the shoreline itself has turned semi-solid as it refracts the flare's corona. It looks like there's flesh down there, a great beast sidling up to the fence.

I walk down and shine my flashlight on them and see that it is flesh. Not one creature, but thousands. Smelt. Thousands and thousands of smelt cozying up to the shore, coming as close as they can to the flame.

I don't notice Suzy until she's gusting sour breath over my shoulder. "The fuck is that?"

"Smelt."

She stands there looking at the fish awhile, spitting into her Coke can.

Then she turns back to her flare, gives it the up-down. For a moment I think she might genuflect.

"Fucking smelt," she scoffs, walking away.

I spend the rest of the shift watching the smelt shudder in the balm of the flare. Thousands of fish inching toward the tail gas column as it roars and rages through the punctured dark. Light licking them silver and bronze, the smelt push and push against the shore—close and closer but never close enough.

I drive home past the wind turbines thinking as I often do about a hundred thousand years from now when maybe someone would come across this place. I talked about this once, with Mum. We walked into a cornfield just to look at the turbines and when we got there I asked what would happen if there were no corn or soy or farmers left, just the turbines marking the graves of fields. How maybe a thousand years from now there would be a new kind of people like *Mad Max* and they wouldn't remember farms or electricity or the nuclear power plant in Kincardine. How these future humans might find this place where turbines sprouted up taller than any trees, their arms like great white whales. The surrounding farms all gone to wild again. And what else would these new people think but that these massive three-armed hangmen were slow-spinning gods? "That's very well put," Mum said then, as if she were the teacher she'd always wanted to be instead of being a woman who answered the phones at NRCore three days a week. She stood beneath that turbine, staring up at its bland white belly for a long time before she finally said, "It does sort of look like a god. A faceless god."

Eileen's still sleeping when I get home so I pour some merlot and head straight down through the oil-reek into the basement. Eileen was right. The smell is getting bad. Detectable from the kitchen and almost unbearable in the basement itself and what this means is a matter of days at most. Below, the morning sun winks and flickers through the cracked foundation. The hole is the size of a truck tire now, and there are more bones floating at the surface. I grab an old broken chair leg and stir the muck around, transfixed by the bones. One that looks like a splintered T-bone, one that may be a gnawed nose, another that I'm pretty sure has part of a fingernail attached. A row of molars like a hardened stitch of corn.

The teenagers. In the yard. The story I've never believed.

"It's all right," Mum would say if she could speak. "It's all right, sweet Sonny Boy. You're all right, you're here, everything's going to be fine."

And Mum would be right. For the moment everything is nice and cool and dark and we sit there in the gentle silence until Mum wants me to tell her some of the old stories so I do. I tell them the way she used to tell me. I tell about her grandfather, the Lambton oil man who sniffed for gushers and got ripped off on the patent for the Canada rig. I tell about the last gusher and the time lightning struck the still and all the dirty land sales the companies made to get things started in Sarnia. Water, I remember her saying once. It was all about water. They chose Sarnia because they needed to be by the river. I tell her the same now and she sits there smiling faintly, a twinkle in her gold incisor and for the moment the two of us are calm and happy and together.

When I creep into bed Eileen wakes up. She reaches for her bedside table, produces a rectangular LED blear. "It's almost noon," she says. "What were you doing?" I tell her I was in the basement. She asks if I was playing *wow* again and I say no just reading some old volumes of *Turok*. She murmurs the usual: just don't take up *Magic* like her brother. I laugh and tell her no, of course not.

Then she rises. Sits up in bed and I can see even with the blackout blinds that she's gone serious. She asks if there's something going on with me lately. I tell her the usual bullshit, just a hard day at work. And how could you expect what comes next:

"You know I'm never going to get better?"

Times like this, I'm not good at saying the right thing because there is no right thing.

"It's just," she continues, "sometimes I forget, myself, that it's not ever going to end, that it's just going to keep going like this for who knows how long. And I just want to be sure that you know the full extent of that."

I tell her yeah, of course.

She squints through the dark. "It's just, I know it's hard for you, and if you ever wanted—"

I tell her no, absolutely not, whatever it is. Whisper that I don't want anything different, don't need anything more than what we have. I go big spoon and nestle into her until I'm hot, until I'm roasting under the blankets and wanting to roll away but also wanting just to melt, to seep, to burn hot as compost in nitrogen night.

The day Dad died, Mum and I sat in the bug tent in the backyard watching a horde of blue jays eat the heads off Mum's sunflowers. Any other day she would have got up and screamed carnage at those birds but she just sat there watching. He'd weighed about forty-five pounds at the end and it was not a nice thing for a wife or a fifteen-year-old son to watch. It ended graciously, in sleep. The ambulance came and Mum went with because there were checks to be done, forms to be signed. After she came home we sat in the backyard watching those ravenous blue jays pick through a row of twenty or thirty six-foot sunflowers. I said how I didn't know blue jays could be so vicious and Mum said oh yeah, everything beautiful has a dark side, just like everything wretched has a loveliness. When there were only three heads remaining and the blue jays were pecking tiredly, half of them gone, Mum told me those sunflowers had been growing in the spot where she'd buried her placenta after I was born. She said she'd always figured that's why they grew so well there. Said how the placenta had enriched the soil and so in a way I was feeding those blue jays, we both were. And so the two of us sat there watching the birds gobble up the vegetation we'd nourished together and I saw each one grow a face. The last three sunflowers became me and Dad and

Mum and I watched the blue jays shred those yellow faces into mangled tufts.

I take the long way to work and when I see the wind turbines I find myself driving toward them. Driving down a farm road and then onto a corn farm with a turbine on a strip of grass and weed and I'm leaping out of the car and sprinting up to it, kneeling while this terrible white demiurge churns its arms in slow rotation. I kneel there thinking up toward that turbine and feeling overpowered by something blunt and terrible and awesome. The sound of the thing is huge and steady and sonorous, an Olympian didgeridoo, and I remember about the bats. How this strange hum draws them in and then the arms send them plummeting into the fields where the farmers have to burn them so they don't attract pests. The arms spin slow but in their slowness there's something massive, something enormous and indifferent and nearly perfect. I imagine myself chopped into atoms, into confetti. I see tiny particles of my hair and skin feathering over the field, blending with the earth and the soil, becoming vegetable, becoming corn. The wholeness of that resignation, a longing to be unmade, to wilt beyond worry and debt, pension and disease.

The farmer whizzes over on an ATV. Behind the quad there's a trailer carrying a blue chemical drum, the skull-and-crossbones symbol on the side. The farmer asks if I'm all right and I tell him sure, fine, never better.

"Well then," he says.

I walk away wondering how much ethanol's in the soil.

—

The night shift sags and sputters. Clouds brood and curdle over the river. I get a text from Eileen saying she's smelling that oil-smell again and is she going insane. I text back not to worry, it's just the construction, I'll phone the city tomorrow. I tell myself don't check the phone don't check the phone and then I check and it says that Eileen's brother's on the way.

What I do is panic. What I do is leave, which is a fireable offence. What I do is vacate my coveralls there in the middle of the unit with Suzy walking through shouting don't even think about it but I need to get home and so I just say, "Be right back" and hustle to my car without even showering.

What I do is drive tilting and teetering and when I get home there's a cruiser in the driveway among the shadowy hulks of graders and loaders lurking against the orange plastic mesh. Eileen's in her chair at the top of the stairs saying sorry, she had to, her brother saw what was downstairs. She looks at me, a little broken.

"I'm sorry."

"It's okay. It's weird, super weird. But I love you. We can talk about it."

I head down into the basement where a redheaded cop and Eileen's brother stand kneeling over the muskeg pit, their backs to Mum. They've moved her slightly, pulled her beneath the stark light of the pull-string bulb. Up close, she looks bad. Wrinkly and purplish, with a sickly glaze.

I reach out to embrace her and the cop says no, don't, you can't do that. I ask him am I under arrest and he says you watch too much TV but this is basically unprecedented and we're going to have to ask you a few questions downtown.

I nod to Mum: "What'll happen to her?"

The cop winces. "Probably have to confiscate the body. Evidence."

So I don't let go. I don't consult the cop. I step closer and hug Mum tight, press my face against hers and kiss both cheeks. Pull away and look deep into her face, which has been in the shadows but is visible now, a snaggle of resin and vein.

My pocket beeps. A text from Suzy: "The fuck are you? Get back here emergency all hands."

Unlike feathered or furred animals, the human is a particularly difficult creature to preserve via taxidermy or other means. The main concern is the fragility of human skin, which discolours strikingly and stretches much more than animal skin. The taxidermied human, in other words, becomes highly unsightly. Take Jeremy Bentham's failed auto-icon experiment, in which his otherwise soundly preserved head acquired a ghastly appearance and after years of student pranks had to be hidden away in a cupboard. While it is something of a legal grey area, it is also generally frowned upon, morally, to taxidermy or otherwise mount a human body. And yet experiments continue, mummification goes on, glassy eyes stare back unblinking from the far side of basement walls.

The enunciator's going Class A and everyone's running around frantic as I scramble into my coveralls and grab an SCBA and head out to Tower #1. Sal's walking away from the scene, heading for the parking lot. "Fuck this," he grumbles into his SCBA helmet. "Not worth it."

I ignore him, keep going, suddenly beyond worry, over fear. When I look up I can see a red alert light blinking by the broiler on Tower #1, so I head over and climb the stairs.

Suzy's down below and shouting, "Back inside back inside" but she can't be talking to me because I'm floating. Floating very slowly, the world turned heavy and blurry. There's a strange heat and a blur in the air and Suzy's shouting, "Inside inside" but now I'm starting to think she might be shouting "Sulfide," is clearly shouting "Sulfide." Which seems funny. Which seems hilarious. Which seems perfect.

The enunciator ratchets up a notch, becomes a didgeridoo.

Below, the hydrants swivel their R2-D2 heads and let loose. Twenty hydrants sending millions of gallons of water arcing through the air to knock the gas off and that, too, is hilarious.

In the distance, turbines churn and churn and churn like children's pinwheels, blowing all the bad air far far away.

I keep climbing. The hydrants arc and spit and soak me. I slip on the latticed steel stairs and recover and get to the valve near the alert light, start to turn it but it's heavy, wildly heavy. Comically heavy as I lean in and stagger a little and then get it turning, get it shut.

On the way back to the stairs my legs are bendy like bubble gum. I take a step and then wilt into a kind of human puddle. Writhing onto my stomach, I see through the platform's steel grid two ambulances and a fire truck raging into the parking lot. My SCBA's bleating like a duck or a bulldozer and in the distance there are sirens, beautiful sirens. The hydrants spit their applause, twenty tearful arcs of triumph.

Eileen appears beside me, flapping turbine arms. I move to speak her name but she shushes me, fern-teeth wavering in the bog of her mouth. Her tongue is a hundred sea-snakes and she's saying shush, never mind, she's come to take me away. As I'm clutching the nubs on her scaly green withers, I ask what happened to Mum, to the basement muskeg. She tells me diverted pipeline and the company will pay us off and Mum's all right now, it's time to let her go. And of course she's right, Eileen. Of course she's always been perfect and right and brave, so brave.

She starts to flap her turbine wings and soon we're chugging up and soaring, cruising, swooping high over the river, the hydrants swirling through the sky below. Eileen curls into a loop-de-loop and when we come back up I can see that the hydrants have become gushers. Twenty black fountains arcing and curling through the floodlit night. Down below, a million neon-blue smelt dance calypso at the surface of the river. Mum stands beneath the bridge, looking up and waving, her face no longer discoloured, her gold incisor gleaming.

I glance over at Eileen, green eyes glowing elfin and wild. I tell her I have something to confess and she says she knows, she always knew. She says it's a little weird, the thing with me and Mum, but what isn't a little weird?

We catch hold of a thermal that takes us up fast, too fast, high above the black arcs of the fountains. The air strobes and changes colour and Eileen twirls a wing and says, "Look." What I see is a sky full of plants. Coral and krill and strange ancient grasses and we're riding it, soaring on the spirits of five hundred million years and for once it is not bad, is not sickening. All around us the gleaming ghosts of sedge and bulrushes, zooplankton and anemones, and all of it pulsing green again. Below the river full of dancing neon smelt as Eileen spreads her wings and jags her beak and tells me it was true, was always true: we were all compost, all along. I tell her thank you and I love you, cling to her wings as we rise up burning through the broken brilliant sky.

ABOUT THE CONTRIBUTORS

Michela Carrière is an Indigenous adventurer and artist from the trapline sixty kilometres from Cumberland House, Saskatchewan. She has grown up learning from her parents and grandparents, who have lived in this area for generations, practising the Cree way of life. She is now actively learning traditional medicine as she pursues the path of a Cree herbalist. Passing on her knowledge and experience through her company, Aski Holistic Adventures, she guides people on healing adventures in the wild nature of the north, on the homelands of the Cree and Métis.

Paola Ferrante's debut poetry collection, *What to Wear When Surviving a Lion Attack* (Mansfield Press, 2019), was shortlisted for the 2020 Gerald Lampert Memorial Award. She won *The New Quarterly*'s 2019 Peter Hinchcliffe Fiction Award and *Room* magazine's 2018 prize for Fiction. Her work has appeared in *PRISM international*, *Joyland*, *The Puritan*, *Grain*, *The Fiddlehead*, and elsewhere. She is the poetry editor at *Minola Review* and is currently working on her first collection of short fiction, *Her Body Among Animals*. She resides in Toronto, Canada.

Lisa Foad's short story collection, *The Night Is a Mouth* (Exile Editions, 2009), won the ReLit Award for Short Fiction and a Writers' Trust of Canada Dayne Ogilvie Honour of Distinction. Her work has appeared in *Taddle Creek*, *ELQ Magazine*, *Poetry Is Dead*, and elsewhere, and has been awarded the Carter V. Cooper Short Fiction Prize. She holds an M.F.A. in fiction from Columbia University, where she was the recipient of a Felipe P. De Alba Fellowship and a nominee for the Henfield Prize. She lives in Toronto, and is currently working on a novel and short story collection.

David Huebert's work has won the CBC Short Story Prize, *The Walrus* Poetry Prize, and was a National Magazine Award nominee (fiction) in 2018 and 2019. David's fiction debut, *Peninsula Sinking*, won the Jim Connors Dartmouth Book Award, was shortlisted for the Alistair MacLeod Short Fiction Prize, and was runner-up for the Danuta Gleed Literary Award. David has taught creative writing at Dalhousie University and is the 2020–2021 Writer in Residence at the University of New Brunswick. His second book of fiction, *Chemical Valley*, is forthcoming from Biblioasis.

Jessica Johns is a Nehiyaw-English-Irish aunty and member of Sucker Creek First Nation in Treaty 8 Territory in Northern Alberta. She is the managing editor for *Room* magazine and a co-organizer of the Indigenous Brilliance Reading Series. Her short story "The Bull of the Cromdale" was nominated for a 2019 National Magazine Award in fiction and her debut poetry chapbook, *How Not to Spill*, won the 2019 bpNichol Chapbook Award. "Bad Cree" won a silver medal for fiction at the 2020 National Magazine Awards.

Rachael Lesosky is a writer from the Okanagan Valley. In 2017, she was a poetry finalist for *The Malahat Review*'s Open Season Awards, and in 2018 she was longlisted for the Jacob Zilber Prize for Short Fiction. Her work can be found in *The Malahat Review* and *Saltern Magazine*. She holds a B.A. in creative writing from the University of Victoria.

Canisia Lubrin is the author of *Voodoo Hypothesis* (Wolsak & Wynn, 2017) and *The Dyzgraph*ˣ*st* (McClelland & Stewart, 2020).

An editor, critic, and teacher, her writing has been published and anthologized internationally, with translations into Spanish, Italian, French, and German. Lubrin's fiction has been shortlisted for the Toronto Book Award and longlisted for The Journey Prize. She was 2019 Writer in Residence at Queen's University and taught poetry at the Banff Centre. *NOW Magazine* featured Lubrin in its 2020 Black Futures issue. In 2018 she was named a writer to watch by the CBC. "The Origin of the Lullaby" is part of her forthcoming linked short story collection, *Code Noir*. She holds an M.F.A. from the University of Guelph.

Born in Montreal and raised in Cobourg, Ontario, **Florence MacDonald** was a practising physician in the Northwest Territories, Hong Kong, and East Africa before becoming a full-time writer. Her multi-award-winning and internationally produced plays include *Elevator*, *Take Care of Me*, *Belle*, *Home is My Road*, *Missing* and *How Do I Love Thee?* With choreographer Shawn Byfield, she co-created the Dora Award–winning tap dance show, *i think i can*. She has written for CBC Radio and her short stories appear in *Understorey Magazine*, *The Fiddlehead*, and *The Dalhousie Review*. Florence is currently working on her novel, *My Heart and I*.

Cara Marks is a writer from Vancouver Island. She earned her B.A. and M.A. in creative writing at the University of Victoria and the University of East Anglia (U.K.). She writes playful, intimate stories, which have been longlisted for the 2018 Carter V. Cooper Short Fiction Competition, the 2017 Australian Book Review's Elizabeth Jolley Short Story Prize, and the 2016 Mogford Prize for Food and Drink Writing. Her work has appeared in the Commonwealth Writers' literary journal, *adda*, and elsewhere. As part of her creative-critical

Ph.D. on food, literature and empathy, she is currently writing her first novel.

Fawn Parker is president of The Parker Agency and co-founder of *BAD NUDES Magazine*. She is the author of *Set-Point* (ARP Books, 2019), *Jolie-Laide* (Palimpsest, 2021), and *Dumb-Show* (ARP Books, 2021). Her work has been published in *EVENT*, *The Puritan*, *All Lit Up*, and *Maisonneuve Magazine*. She is the recipient of the Irving Layton Award for Fiction, the Avie Bennett Emerging Writers Scholarship, and the Adam Penn Gilders Award for Creative Writing. She is currently working on her third and fourth novels.

Susan Sanford Blades holds an M.F.A. in fiction from the University of Victoria. Her stories have appeared in *Cosmonauts Avenue*, *Minola Review*, *the moth: arts and literature*, *Southwest Review*, *The Puritan*, *Numéro Cinq*, *Coming Attractions 16*, and other publications. "The Rest of Him" is an excerpt from her novel, *Fake It So Real*, that will be published by Nightwood Editions in fall 2020. Susan lives with her three sons in Victoria, B.C., where she is working on her second novel.

John Elizabeth Stintzi is a novelist and poet who grew up on a cattle farm in northwestern Ontario. In 2019, they were awarded the Writers' Trust of Canada's RBC Bronwen Wallace Award for Emerging Writers, as well as *The Malahat Review*'s Long Poem Prize. Their work has appeared in the *Kenyon Review*, *Fiddlehead*, *The Malahat Review*, and *Ploughshares*. They are the author of the novel *Vanishing Monuments* (Arsenal Pulp Press, 2020), as well as the poetry collection *Junebat* (House of Anansi, 2020). They currently live and work in the United States.

Hsien Chong Tan was born in Singapore and holds an M.F.A. from the New Writers Project at the University of Texas at Austin. "The Last Snow Globe Repairman in the World" was the winner of *PRISM international*'s 2019 Jacob Zilber Prize for Short Fiction and was shortlisted for a 2020 National Magazine Award. Hsien's stories have also appeared in *Mid-American Review*, *Crab Orchard Review*, and elsewhere. He lives in Vancouver with his wife and cats, and is currently working on a collection of short stories.

For more information about the publications that submitted to this year's competition, The Journey Prize, and *The Journey Prize Stories*, please visit www.facebook.com/TheJourneyPrize.

The Dalhousie Review is an award-winning literary journal published triannually by Dalhousie University. Now in its one hundredth year, it features poetry, fiction, essays, and interviews by both established and emerging writers in Canada and from around the world as well as reviews of recent books, films, albums, and performances. Past contributors include some of Canada's most celebrated writers, such as Margaret Atwood, Alfred Bailey, Earle Birney, Elizabeth Brewster, Charles Bruce, George Elliott Clarke, Fred Cogswell, Laurence Dakin, Leo Kennedy, A.M. Klein, Kenneth Leslie, Malcolm Lowry, Hugh MacLennan, Alistair MacLeod, Alden Nowlan, A.J.M. Smith, Alice Mackenzie Swaim, W.D. Valgardson, Guy Vanderhaeghe, and Miriam Waddington. Editor: Anthony Enns. Production Manager: Lynne Evans. Correspondence: *The Dalhousie Review*, c/o Dalhousie University, Halifax, NS, B3H 4R2. For subscription and submission guidelines, please contact the Production Manager at Dalhousie.Review@dal.ca

EVENT has inspired and nurtured writers for almost five decades. Featuring the very best in contemporary writing from Canada and abroad, *EVENT* consistently publishes award-winning fiction, poetry, non-fiction, notes on writing, and critical reviews—all topped off by stunning Canadian cover art and illustrations. Stories first published in *EVENT* regularly appear in the *Best Canadian Stories* and *Journey Prize Stories* anthologies, are finalists at the National Magazine Awards, and won the Grand Prix Best Literature and Art Story at the 2017 Canadian Magazine Awards. *EVENT* is also home to Canada's longest-running non-fiction contest (fall deadline), and its Reading Service for Writers. Editor: Shashi Bhat. Managing Editor: Ian Cockfield. Fiction Editor: Christine Dewar. Correspondence: *EVENT*, P.O. Box 2503, New Westminster, BC, V3L 5B2. Email (queries only): event@douglascollege.ca Website: www.eventmagazine.ca

Exile: The Literary Quarterly, established in 1972, is a literary and visual arts magazine that over the years has had writers appear in *The Journey Prize* anthology, including one winner. The magazine also administers the $15,000 Carter V. Cooper Short Fiction Competition, open to Canadian writers only, with two prizes awarded by way of an endowment established by philanthropist Gloria Vanderbilt: $10,000 for best story by an emerging writer and $5,000 for best story by a writer at any point of their career (open call for submissions from May through November). The awards gala for the prizes is presented by the Bank of Montreal Financial Group and held at First Canadian Place in Toronto. Websites: ExileQuarterly.com and TheExcelsisGroup.org

The Fiddlehead, Atlantic Canada's longest-running literary journal, publishes short fiction, poetry, creative non-fiction, and book reviews. It appears four times a year and sponsors three contests (in short fiction, poetry, and creative non-fiction)

that award a total of $6,000 in prizes. *The Fiddlehead* is open to good writing in English or translations into English from all over the world and in a variety of styles, including experimental genres. Editor: Sue Sinclair. Submissions and correspondence: Submittable or mail to *The Fiddlehead*, Campus House, 11 Garland Court, University of New Brunswick, P.O. Box 4400, Fredericton, NB, E3B 5A3. Email (queries only): fiddlehd@unb.ca Website:www.thefiddlehead.ca Twitter: @TheFiddlehd You can also find *The Fiddlehead* on Facebook.

Grain, the journal of eclectic writing, is a literary quarterly out of Saskatchewan—Treaty 4 and Treaty 6 Territories, and the Homeland of the Métis—publishing engaging and challenging writing by Canadian and international writers since 1973. Every issue features new writing from both developing and established writers, and highlights the unique artwork of a different visual artist. Each fall issue features the winning stories and poems from our annual Short *Grain* Contest, judged each year by prominent writers from the Canadian literary community. The two pieces selected from *Grain* for inclusion in this year's *Journey Prize Stories* were originally published in our Indigenous Writers and Storytellers issue (Summer 2019), guest edited by Lisa Bird-Wilson (Guest Fiction and Nonfiction Editor) and Tenille K. Campbell (Guest Poetry Editor). *Grain* is published by the Saskatchewan Writers' Guild in Regina and printed and bound by Houghton Boston in Saskatoon. Editor: Nicole Hadoupis. Associate Fiction and Nonfiction Editor: Lisa Bird-Wilson. Associate Poetry Editor: Alasdair Rees. Correspondence: *Grain* Magazine, P.O. Box 3986, Regina, SK, S4P 3R9. Email: grainmag@skwriter.com Fax: 306 565 8554

Website: www.grainmagazine.ca Twitter/Instagram/Facebook: @GrainLitMag

Based on the idea that fiction is an international movement supported by local communities, **Joyland** is a literary magazine that selects stories regionally. Our editors work with authors connected to locales across North America, including New York, Los Angeles, and Toronto, as well as places underrepresented in cultural media. Our regional verticals highlight the diversity of voices nationwide, and we are proud to have created a home where all can coexist. Publisher: Michelle Lyn King. Associate Editor: Karina Leon. Managing Editor: Sonia Feigelson. Founders: Emily Schultz, Brian J. Davis. Web Developer: Ross Merriam. Section Editors: Kyle Lucia Wu, Amy Shearn, Lisa Locascio, Kate Folk, Kathryn Mockler, Rachel Morgenstern-Clarren, Emma Ruddock, Michelle Lyn King, Laura Chow Reeve, Kait Heacock. Website: www.joylandmagazine.com

The Malahat Review is a quarterly journal of contemporary poetry, fiction, and creative non-fiction by emerging and established writers from Canada and abroad. Summer issues feature the winners of the magazine's Novella and Long Poem prizes, held in alternating years; the fall issues feature the winners of the Far Horizons Award for emerging writers, alternating between poetry and fiction each year; the winter issues feature the winners of the Constance Rooke Creative Nonfiction Prize; and the spring issues feature winners of the Open Season Awards in all three genres (poetry, fiction, and creative non-fiction). All issues feature covers by noted Canadian visual artists and include reviews of Canadian books. Editor: Iain Higgins. Managing Editor: L'Amour Lisik. Correspondence: *The Malahat Review*, University of Victoria, P.O. Box 1800, Station CSC, Victoria, BC, V8W 3H5. Unsolicited submissions and contest entries are accepted through Submittable only (please review guidelines before entering). Email: malahat@uvic.ca Website: www.malahatreview.ca Twitter: @malahatreview Facebook: TheMalahatReview Instagram: malahatreview

PRISM international is a quarterly magazine out of Vancouver, British Columbia, whose office is located on the traditional, ancestral, and unceded territory of the xʷməθkʷəy̓əm people. Our mandate is to publish the best in contemporary writing and translation from Canada and around the world. Writing from *PRISM* has been featured in *Best American Stories*, *Best American Essays*, and *The Journey Prize Stories*, among other noted publications. *PRISM* strives to uplift and shine a light on emerging and established voices across Canada and internationally, and is especially committed to providing a platform for folks who have been systematically marginalized in the literary community, including but not limited to BIPOC groups, cis women, trans women and men, nonbinary people, people with disabilities, and members of the LGBTQ2S community. Prose Editor: Emma Cleary. Poetry Editor: Molly Cross-Blanchard. Executive Editors: Shristi Uprety and Kate Black. Reviews Editor: Cara Nelissen. Submissions and Correspondence: *PRISM international*, Creative Writing Program, The University of British Columbia, Buchanan E462 – 1866 Main Mall, Vancouver, BC, V6T 1Z1. Website: www.prismmagazine.ca

The Puritan began in 2007 and is now an online magazine run from Toronto. *The Puritan* seeks to publish the best in all forms of writing and has published or interviewed some of Canada's most exciting authors. The poetry and fiction *The Puritan* publishes is representative of the best in contemporary writing. The magazine also prides itself on its essays, interviews, and reviews: in-depth, expansive, and engaging discussions of Canadian and global literature. In 2012, *The Puritan* inaugurated its first contest, The Thomas Morton Memorial Prize in Literary Excellence. In 2013, *The Puritan* launched its sister site, *The Town Crier.* The blog has served as a hub of criticism and commentary, connecting a community of writers, readers, and commentators through social media, and focusing on the interplay of literary opinion in and around the city of Toronto. Editor-in-Chief: Puneet Dutt. Managing Editor: Kirstie Turco. Publisher: Jason Freure. Poetry Editor: A. Light Zachary. Essays Editors: Kailey Havelock and Nellwyn Lampert. Interviews Editor: Cho Min. Reviews Editors: Kelly Whitehead and Emilie Kneifel. Website: puritan-magazine.com

Room magazine publishes fiction, poetry, creative non-fiction, and artwork by and about women. *Room* was founded in 1975 (as *Room of One's Own*) to provide opportunities for emerging and established writers and artists who identify as women (cisgender and transgender), transgender men, Two-Spirit, and nonbinary people to publish their work in Canada. Contributors have included some of Canada's most celebrated writers, including Alice Munro, Jane Urquhart, Larissa Lai, Carol Shields, Karen Solie, Pamela Porter, Elizabeth Bachinsky, and Betsy Warland. Each quarter we publish original, thought-provoking works that reflect strength, sensuality, vulnerability, and wit. Correspondence: *Room* magazine, Box 46160 Station D, Vancouver, BC, V6J 5G5. Submissions: roommagazine.com/submit Website: roommagazine.com Email: contactus@roommagazine.com

Taddle Creek often is asked to define itself and, just as often, it tends to refuse to do so. But it will say this: each issue of the magazine contains a multitude of things between its snazzily illustrated covers, including, but not limited to, fiction, poetry, comics, art, interviews, and feature stories. It's an odd mix, to be sure, which is why *Taddle Creek* refers to itself somewhat oddly as a "general-interest literary magazine." Work presented in *Taddle Creek* is humorous, poignant, ephemeral, urban, and rarely overly earnest, though not usually all at once. *Taddle Creek* takes its mission to be the journal for those who detest everything the literary magazine has become in the twenty-first century very seriously. Editor-in-Chief: Conan Tobias. Correspondence: *Taddle Creek*, P.O. Box 611, Station P, Toronto, ON, M5S 2Y4. Email: editor@taddlecreekmag.com. Website: taddlecreekmag.com

Submissions were also received from the following publications:

Agnes and True
(Toronto, ON)
www.agnesandtrue.com

Augur Magazine
(Toronto, ON)
www.augurmag.com

Blank Spaces
blankspaces.alannarusnak
.com

carte blanche
(Montreal, QC)
www.carte-blanche.org

*The CVC Short Fiction
Anthology*
(Toronto, ON)
www.exileeditions.com

FreeFall Magazine
(Calgary, AB)
www.freefallmagazine.ca

*The Group of Seven
Reimagined*
(Victoria, BC)
www.heritagehouse.ca

Hart House Review
(Toronto, ON)
www.harthousereview.ca

The Humber Literary Review
(Toronto, ON)
www.humberliteraryreview
.com

*Invisible Publishing / Sarah
Selecky Writing School*
(Picton, ON)
www.invisiblepublishing.com

Maisonneuve Magazine
(Montreal, QC)
www.maisonneuve.org

Minola Review
(Toronto, ON)
www.minolareview.com

The New Quarterly
(Waterloo, ON)
www.tnq.ca

On Spec
(Edmonton, AB)
www.onspec.ca

Plenitude Magazine
(Victoria, BC)
www.plenitudemagazine.ca

Prairie Fire
(Winnipeg, MB)
www.prairiefire.ca

Pulp Literature
(Richmond, BC)
www.pulpliterature.com

*Release Any Words Stuck
Inside of You II*
(Saskatoon, SK)
www.applebeardeditions.ca

Riddle Fence
(St. John's, NL)
www.riddlefence.com

The /tƐmz/ Review
(London, ON)
www.thetemzreview.com

This Magazine
(Toronto, ON)
www.this.org

The Walrus
(Toronto, ON)
www.thewalrus.ca

PREVIOUS CONTRIBUTING AUTHORS

* Winners of the $10,000 Journey Prize
** Co-winners of the $10,000 Journey Prize

I

1989

SELECTED WITH ALISTAIR MACLEOD

Ven Begamudré, "Word Games"
David Bergen, "Where You're From"
Lois Braun, "The Pumpkin-Eaters"
Constance Buchanan, "Man with Flying Genitals"
Ann Copeland, "Obedience"
Marion Douglas, "Flags"
Frances Itani, "An Evening in the Café"
Diane Keating, "The Crying Out"
Thomas King, "One Good Story, That One"
Holley Rubinsky, "Rapid Transits"*
Jean Rysstad, "Winter Baby"
Kevin Van Tighem, "Whoopers"
M.G. Vassanji, "In the Quiet of a Sunday Afternoon"
Bronwen Wallace, "Chicken 'N' Ribs"
Armin Wiebe, "Mouse Lake"
Budge Wilson, "Waiting"

2

1990

SELECTED WITH LEON ROOKE; GUY VANDERHAEGHE

André Alexis, "Despair: Five Stories of Ottawa"
Glen Allen, "The Hua Guofeng Memorial Warehouse"
Marusia Bociurkiw, "Mama, Donya"
Virgil Burnett, "Billfrith the Dreamer"
Margaret Dyment, "Sacred Trust"
Cynthia Flood, "My Father Took a Cake to France"*
Douglas Glover, "Story Carved in Stone"
Terry Griggs, "Man with the Axe"
Rick Hillis, "Limbo River"

Thomas King, "The Dog I Wish I Had, I Would Call It Helen"
K.D. Miller, "Sunrise Till Dark"
Jennifer Mitton, "Let Them Say"
Lawrence O'Toole, "Goin' to Town with Katie Ann"
Kenneth Radu, "A Change of Heart"
Jenifer Sutherland, "Table Talk"
Wayne Tefs, "Red Rock and After"

3
1991
SELECTED WITH JANE URQUHART

Donald Aker, "The Invitation"
Anton Baer, "Yukon"
Allan Barr, "A Visit from Lloyd"
David Bergen, "The Fall"
Rai Berzins, "Common Sense"
Diana Hartog, "Theories of Grief"
Diane Keating, "The Salem Letters"
Yann Martel, "The Facts Behind the Helsinki Roccamatios"*
Jennifer Mitton, "Polaroid"
Sheldon Oberman, "This Business with Elijah"
Lynn Podgurny, "Till Tomorrow, Maple Leaf Mills"
James Riseborough, "She Is Not His Mother"
Patricia Stone, "Living on the Lake"

4
1992
SELECTED WITH SANDRA BIRDSELL

David Bergen, "The Bottom of the Glass"
Maria A. Billion, "No Miracles Sweet Jesus"
Judith Cowan, "By the Big River"
Steven Heighton, "How Beautiful upon the Mountains"
Steven Heighton, "A Man Away from Home Has No Neighbours"
L. Rex Kay, "Travelling"
Rozena Maart, "No Rosa, No District Six"*
Guy Malet De Carteret, "Rainy Day"
Carmelita McGrath, "Silence"
Michael Mirolla, "A Theory of Discontinuous Existence"
Diane Juttner Perreault, "Bella's Story"
Eden Robinson, "Traplines"

5

1993

SELECTED WITH GUY VANDERHAEGHE

Caroline Adderson, "Oil and Dread"
David Bergen, "La Rue Prevette"
Marina Endicott, "With the Band"
Dayv James-French, "Cervine"
Michael Kenyon, "Durable Tumblers"
K.D. Miller, "A Litany in Time of Plague"
Robert Mullen, "Flotsam"
Gayla Reid, "Sister Doyle's Men"*
Oakland Ross, "Bang-bang"
Robert Sherrin, "Technical Battle for Trial Machine"
Carol Windley, "The Etruscans"

6

1994

SELECTED WITH DOUGLAS GLOVER;
JUDITH CHANT (CHAPTERS)

Anne Carson, "Water Margins: An Essay on Swimming by My Brother"
Richard Cumyn, "The Sound He Made"
Genni Gunn, "Versions"
Melissa Hardy, "Long Man the River"*
Robert Mullen, "Anomie"
Vivian Payne, "Free Falls"
Jim Reil, "Dry"
Robyn Sarah, "Accept My Story"
Joan Skogan, "Landfall"
Dorothy Speak, "Relatives in Florida"
Alison Wearing, "Notes from Under Water"

7

1995

SELECTED WITH M.G. VASSANJI;
RICHARD BACHMANN (A DIFFERENT DRUMMER BOOKS)

Michelle Alfano, "Opera"
Mary Borsky, "Maps of the Known World"
Gabriella Goliger, "Song of Ascent"
Elizabeth Hay, "Hand Games"
Shaena Lambert, "The Falling Woman"
Elise Levine, "Boy"

Roger Burford Mason, "The Rat-Catcher's Kiss"
Antanas Sileika, "Going Native"
Kathryn Woodward, "Of Marranos and Gilded Angels"*

8
1996
SELECTED WITH OLIVE SENIOR;
BEN McNALLY (NICHOLAS HOARE LTD.)

Rick Bowers, "Dental Bytes"
David Elias, "How I Crossed Over"
Elyse Gasco, "Can You Wave Bye Bye, Baby?"*
Danuta Gleed, "Bones"
Elizabeth Hay, "The Friend"
Linda Holeman, "Turning the Worm"
Elaine Littman, "The Winner's Circle"
Murray Logan, "Steam"
Rick Maddocks, "Lessons from the Sputnik Diner"
K.D. Miller, "Egypt Land"
Gregor Robinson, "Monster Gaps"
Alma Subasic, "Dust"

9
1997
SELECTED WITH NINO RICCI; NICHOLAS PASHLEY
(UNIVERSITY OF TORONTO BOOKSTORE)

Brian Bartlett, "Thomas, Naked"
Dennis Bock, "Olympia"
Kristen den Hartog, "Wave"
Gabriella Goliger, "Maladies of the Inner Ear"**
Terry Griggs, "Momma Had a Baby"
Mark Anthony Jarman, "Righteous Speedboat"
Judith Kalman, "Not for Me a Crown of Thorns"
Andrew Mullins, "The World of Science"
Sasenarine Persaud, "Canada Geese and Apple Chatney"
Anne Simpson, "Dreaming Snow"**
Sarah Withrow, "Ollie"
Terence Young, "The Berlin Wall"

10
1998
SELECTED BY PETER BUITENHUIS; HOLLEY RUBINSKY;
CELIA DUTHIE (DUTHIE BOOKS LTD.)

John Brooke, "The Finer Points of Apples"*
Ian Colford, "The Reason for the Dream"
Libby Creelman, "Cruelty"
Michael Crummey, "Serendipity"
Stephen Guppy, "Downwind"
Jane Eaton Hamilton, "Graduation"
Elise Levine, "You Are You Because Your Little Dog Loves You"
Jean McNeil, "Bethlehem"
Liz Moore, "Eight-Day Clock"
Edward O'Connor, "The Beatrice of Victoria College"
Tim Rogers, "Scars and Other Presents"
Denise Ryan, "Marginals, Vivisections, and Dreams"
Madeleine Thien, "Simple Recipes"
Cheryl Tibbetts, "Flowers of Africville"

11
1999
SELECTED BY LESLEY CHOYCE; SHELDON CURRIE;
MARY-JO ANDERSON (FROG HOLLOW BOOKS)

Mike Barnes, "In Florida"
Libby Creelman, "Sunken Island"
Mike Finigan, "Passion Sunday"
Jane Eaton Hamilton, "Territory"
Mark Anthony Jarman, "Travels into Several Remote Nations of the
    World"
Barbara Lambert, "Where the Bodies Are Kept"
Linda Little, "The Still"
Larry Lynch, "The Sitter"
Sandra Sabatini, "The One with the News"
Sharon Steams, "Brothers"
Mary Walters, "Show Jumping"
Alissa York, "The Back of the Bear's Mouth"*

12

2000

SELECTED BY CATHERINE BUSH; HAL NIEDZVIECKI;
MARC GLASSMAN (PAGES BOOKS AND MAGAZINES)

Andrew Gray, "The Heart of the Land"

Lee Henderson, "Sheep Dub"

Jessica Johnson, "We Move Slowly"

John Lavery, "The Premier's New Pyjamas"

J.A. McCormack, "Hearsay"

Nancy Richler, "Your Mouth Is Lovely"

Andrew Smith, "Sightseeing"

Karen Solie, "Onion Calendar"

Timothy Taylor, "Doves of Townsend"*

Timothy Taylor, "Pope's Own"

Timothy Taylor, "Silent Cruise"

R.M. Vaughan, "Swan Street"

13

2001

SELECTED BY ELYSE GASCO; MICHAEL HELM;
MICHAEL NICHOLSON (INDIGO BOOKS & MUSIC INC.)

Kevin Armstrong, "The Cane Field"*

Mike Barnes, "Karaoke Mon Amour"

Heather Birrell, "Machaya"

Heather Birrell, "The Present Perfect"

Craig Boyko, "The Gun"

Vivette J. Kady, "Anything That Wiggles"

Billie Livingston, "You're Taking All the Fun Out of It"

Annabel Lyon, "Fishes"

Lisa Moore, "The Way the Light Is"

Heather O'Neill, "Little Suitcase"

Susan Rendell, "In the Chambers of the Sea"

Tim Rogers, "Watch"

Margrith Schraner, "Dream Dig"

14

2002

SELECTED BY ANDRÉ ALEXIS;
DEREK McCORMACK; DIANE SCHOEMPERLEN

Mike Barnes, "Cogagwee"

Geoffrey Brown, "Listen"

Jocelyn Brown, "Miss Canada"*

Emma Donoghue, "What Remains"

Jonathan Goldstein, "You Are a Spaceman with Your Head Under the
   Bathroom Stall Door"

Robert McGill, "Confidence Men"

Robert McGill, "The Stars Are Falling"

Nick Melling, "Philemon"

Robert Mullen, "Alex the God"

Karen Munro, "The Pool"

Leah Postman, "Being Famous"

Neil Smith, "Green Fluorescent Protein"

15

2003

SELECTED BY MICHELLE BERRY;
TIMOTHY TAYLOR; MICHAEL WINTER

Rosaria Campbell, "Reaching"

Hilary Dean, "The Lemon Stories"

Dawn Rae Downton, "Hansel and Gretel"

Anne Fleming, "Gay Dwarves of America"

Elyse Friedman, "Truth"

Charlotte Gill, "Hush"

Jessica Grant, "My Husband's Jump"*

Jacqueline Honnet, "Conversion Classes"

S.K. Johannesen, "Resurrection"

Avner Mandelman, "Cuckoo"

Tim Mitchell, "Night Finds Us"

Heather O'Neill, "The Difference Between Me and Goldstein"

16
2004
SELECTED BY ELIZABETH HAY; LISA MOORE; MICHAEL REDHILL

Anar Ali, "Baby Khaki's Wings"
Kenneth Bonert, "Packers and Movers"
Jennifer Clouter, "Benny and the Jets"
Daniel Griffin, "Mercedes Buyer's Guide"
Michael Kissinger, "Invest in the North"
Devin Krukoff, "The Last Spark"*
Elaine McCluskey, "The Watermelon Social"
William Metcalfe, "Nice Big Car, Rap Music Coming Out the Window"
Lesley Millard, "The Uses of the Neckerchief"
Adam Lewis Schroeder, "Burning the Cattle at Both Ends"
Michael V. Smith, "What We Wanted"
Neil Smith, "Isolettes"
Patricia Rose Young, "Up the Clyde on a Bike"

17
2005
SELECTED BY JAMES GRAINGER AND NANCY LEE

Randy Boyagoda, "Rice and Curry Yacht Club"
Krista Bridge, "A Matter of Firsts"
Josh Byer, "Rats, Homosex, Saunas, and Simon"
Craig Davidson, "Failure to Thrive"
McKinley M. Hellenes, "Brighter Thread"
Catherine Kidd, "Green-Eyed Beans"
Pasha Malla, "The Past Composed"
Edward O'Connor, "Heard Melodies Are Sweet"
Barbara Romanik, "Seven Ways into Chandigarh"
Sandra Sabatini, "The Dolphins at Sainte Marie"
Matt Shaw, "Matchbook for a Mother's Hair"*
Richard Simas, "Anthropologies"
Neil Smith, "Scrapbook"
Emily White, "Various Metals"

18

2006

**SELECTED BY STEVEN GALLOWAY;
ZSUZSI GARTNER; ANNABEL LYON**

Heather Birrell, "BriannaSusannaAlana"*

Craig Boyko, "The Baby"

Craig Boyko, "The Beloved Departed"

Nadia Bozak, "Heavy Metal Housekeeping"

Lee Henderson, "Conjugation"

Melanie Little, "Wrestling"

Matthew Rader, "The Lonesome Death of Joseph Fey"

Scott Randall, "Law School"

Sarah Selecky, "Throwing Cotton"

Damian Tarnopolsky, "Sleepy"

Martin West, "Cretacea"

David Whitton, "The Eclipse"

Clea Young, "Split"

19

2007

**SELECTED BY CAROLINE ADDERSON;
DAVID BEZMOZGIS; DIONNE BRAND**

Andrew J. Borkowski, "Twelve Versions of Lech"

Craig Boyko, "OZY"*

Grant Buday, "The Curve of the Earth"

Nicole Dixon, "High-Water Mark"

Krista Foss, "Swimming in Zanzibar"

Pasha Malla, "Respite"

Alice Petersen, "After Summer"

Patricia Robertson, "My Hungarian Sister"

Rebecca Rosenblum, "Chilly Girl"

Nicholas Ruddock, "How Eunice Got Her Baby"

Jean Van Loon, "Stardust"

20
2008
SELECTED BY LYNN COADY; HEATHER O'NEILL; NEIL SMITH

Théodora Armstrong, "Whale Stories"
Mike Christie, "Goodbye Porkpie Hat"
Anna Leventhal, "The Polar Bear at the Museum"
Naomi K. Lewis, "The Guiding Light"
Oscar Martens, "Breaking on the Wheel"
Dana Mills, "Steaming for Godthab"
Saleema Nawaz, "My Three Girls"*
Scott Randall, "The Gifted Class"
S. Kennedy Sobol, "Some Light Down"
Sarah Steinberg, "At Last at Sea"
Clea Young, "Chaperone"

21
2009
SELECTED BY CAMILLA GIBB;
LEE HENDERSON; REBECCA ROSENBLUM

Daniel Griffin, "The Last Great Works of Alvin Cale"
Jesus Hardwell, "Easy Living"
Paul Headrick, "Highlife"
Sarah Keevil, "Pyro"
Adrian Michael Kelly, "Lure"
Fran Kimmel, "Picturing God's Ocean"
Lynne Kutsukake, "Away"
Alexander MacLeod, "Miracle Mile"
Dave Margoshes, "The Wisdom of Solomon"
Shawn Syms, "On the Line"
Sarah L. Taggart, "Deaf"
Yasuko Thanh, "Floating Like the Dead"*

22

2010

SELECTED BY PASHA MALLA; JOAN THOMAS; ALISSA YORK

Carolyn Black, "Serial Love"

Andrew Boden, "Confluence of Spoors"

Laura Boudreau, "The Dead Dad Game"

Devon Code, "Uncle Oscar"*

Danielle Egan, "Publicity"

Krista Foss, "The Longitude of Okay"

Lynne Kutsukake, "Mating"

Ben Lof, "When in the Field with Her at His Back"

Andrew MacDonald, "Eat Fist!"

Eliza Robertson, "Ship's Log"

Mike Spry, "Five Pounds Short and Apologies to Nelson Algren"

Damian Tarnopolsky, "Laud We the Gods"

23

2011

SELECTED BY ALEXANDER MACLEOD;
ALISON PICK; SARAH SELECKY

Jay Brown, "The Girl from the War"

Michael Christie, "The Extra"

Seyward Goodhand, "The Fur Trader's Daughter"

Miranda Hill, "Petitions to Saint Chronic"*

Fran Kimmel, "Laundry Day"

Ross Klatte, "First-Calf Heifer"

Michelle Serwatuk, "My Eyes Are Dim"

Jessica Westhead, "What I Would Say"

Michelle Winters, "Toupée"

D.W. Wilson, "The Dead Roads"

24
2012
SELECTED BY MICHAEL CHRISTIE;
KATHRYN KUITENBROUWER; KATHLEEN WINTER

Kris Bertin, "Is Alive and Can Move"

Shashi Bhat, "Why I Read *Beowulf*"

Astrid Blodgett, "Ice Break"

Trevor Corkum, "You Were Loved"

Nancy Jo Cullen, "Ashes"

Kevin Hardcastle, "To Have to Wait"

Andrew Hood, "I'm Sorry and Thank You"

Andrew Hood, "Manning"

Grace O'Connell, "The Many Faces of Montgomery Clift"

Jasmina Odor, "Barcelona"

Alex Pugsley, "Crisis on Earth-X"*

Eliza Robertson, "Sea Drift"

Martin West, "My Daughter of the Dead Reeds"

25
2013
SELECTED BY MIRANDA HILL;
MARK MEDLEY; RUSSELL WANGERSKY

Steven Benstead, "Megan's Bus"

Jay Brown, "The Egyptians"

Andrew Forbes, "In the Foothills"

Philip Huynh, "Gulliver's Wife"

Amy Jones, "Team Ninja"

Marnie Lamb, "Mrs. Fujimoto's Wednesday Afternoons"

Doretta Lau, "How Does a Single Blade of Grass Thank the Sun?"

Laura Legge, "It's Raining in Paris"

Natalie Morrill, "Ossicles"

Zoey Leigh Peterson, "Sleep World"

Eliza Robertson, "My Sister Sang"

Naben Ruthnum, "Cinema Rex"*

26
2014
**SELECTED BY STEVEN W. BEATTIE;
CRAIG DAVIDSON; SALEEMA NAWAZ**

Rosaria Campbell, "Probabilities"

Nancy Jo Cullen, "Hashtag Maggie Vandermeer"

M.A. Fox, "Piano Boy"

Kevin Hardcastle, "Old Man Marchuk"

Amy Jones, "Wolves, Cigarettes, Gum"

Tyler Keevil, "Sealskin"*

Jeremy Lanaway, "Downturn"

Andrew MacDonald, "Four Minutes"

Lori McNulty, "Monsoon Season"

Shana Myara, "Remainders"

Julie Roorda, "How to Tell If Your Frog Is Dead"

Leona Theis, "High Beams"

Clea Young, "Juvenile"

27
2015
**SELECTED BY ANTHONY DE SA;
TANIS RIDEOUT; CARRIE SNYDER**

Charlotte Bondy, "Renaude"

Emily Bossé, "Last Animal Standing on Gentleman's Farm"

Deirdre Dore, "The Wise Baby"*

Charlie Fiset, "Maggie's Farm"

K'ari Fisher, "Mercy Beatrice Wrestles the Noose"

Anna Ling Kaye, "Red Egg and Ginger"

Andrew MacDonald, "The Perfect Man for My Husband"

Madeleine Maillet, "Achilles' Death"

Lori McNulty, "Fingernecklace"

Sarah Meehan Sirk, "Moonman"

Ron Schafrick, "Lovely Company"

Georgia Wilder, "Cocoa Divine and the Lightning Police"

28
2016
SELECTED BY KATE CAYLEY;
BRIAN FRANCIS; MADELEINE THIEN

Carleigh Baker, "Chins and Elbows"
Paige Cooper, "The Roar"
Charlie Fiset, "If I Ever See the Sun"
Mahak Jain, "The Origin of Jaanvi"
Colette Langlois, "The Emigrants"*
Alex Leslie, "The Person You Want to See"
Andrew MacDonald, "Progress on a Genetic Level"
J.R. McConvey, "Home Range"
J.R. McConvey, "How the Grizzly Came to Hang in the Royal Oak Hotel"
Souvankham Thammavongsa, "Mani Pedi"
Souvankham Thammavongsa, "Paris"

29
2017
SELECTED BY KEVIN HARDCASTLE;
GRACE O'CONNELL; AYELET TSABARI

Lisa Alward, "Old Growth"
Sharon Bala, "Butter Tea at Starbucks"*
Sharon Bala, "Reading Week"
Patrick Doerksen, "Leech"
Sarah Kabamba, "They Come Crying
Michael Meagher, "Used to It"
Darlene Naponse, "She Is Water"
Maria Reva, "Subject Winifred"
Jack Wang, "The Nature of Things"
Kelly Ward, "A Girl and a Dog on a Friday Night"

30
2018
SELECTED BY SHARON BALA;
KERRY CLARE; ZOEY LEIGH PETERSON

Shashi Bhat, "Mute"*
Greg Brown, "Bear"
Greg Brown, "Love"
Alicia Elliott, "Tracks"
Liz Harmer, "Never Prosper"
Philip Huynh, "The Forbidden Purple City"
Jason Jobin, "Before He Left"
Aviva Dale Martin, "Barcelona"
Rowan McCandless, "Castaways"
Sofia Mostaghimi, "Desperada"
Jess Taylor, "Two Sex Addicts Fall in Love"
Iryn Tushabe, "A Separation"
Carly Vandergriendt, "Resurfacing"

31
2019
SELECTED BY CARLEIGH BAKER; CATHERINE HERNANDEZ;
JOSHUA WHITEHEAD

Sarah Christina Brown, "Land of Living Skies"
Kai Conradi, "Every True Artist"
Francesca Ekwuyasi, "Orun Is Heaven"
Jason Jobin, "They Would Pour Us into Boxes"
Hajera Khaja, "Waiting for Adnan"
Ben Ladouceur, "A Boy of Good Breeding"
Angélique Lalonde, "Pooka"*
Michael LaPointe, "Candidate"
Canisia Lubrin, "No ID or We Could Be Brothers"
Samantha Jade Macpherson, "The Fish and the Dragons"
Troy Sebastian/nupqu ʔakɬam̓, "Tax Niʔ Pik̓ak (A Long Time Ago)"
Leanne Toshiko Simpson, "Monsters"